LIVING IN TURMOIL

A Red Asscher Thriller

P. C. Chinick

A Russian Hill Press Book
United States • United Kingdom • Australia

R̶H̶P̶
Russian Hill Press

Living in Turmoil is a work of historical fiction. Apart from the well-known actual people, events and locales that figure in the narrative, all names, characters, places and incidences are the products of the author's imagination or are used factiously. Any resemblance to current events or locales, or to living persons, is entirely coincidental.

Library of Congress Control Number: 2016906644

ISBN: 978-0-9911973-3-0
eISBN: 978-0-9911973-2-3

To all of those who played a part in getting
this novel published. Thank you all!

LIVING IN TURMOIL

ONE
Central China 1943

ANYA PAVLOVITCH CLENCHED HER JAW. EVERY muscle in her body tightened as she scanned the overcast sky. A single engine airplane sputtered overhead. The underside of each wing revealed large red dots, reminiscent of a black widow. It was too late to pray.

"Tojo," Mac Benson said. "It's a one-manned Japanese fighter. He's probably on a scouting mission."

"We're all dressed in peasant garb aboard a sampan," her friend and guide Bia said. "From that height he'll assume we're fishermen." Bia's husband maneuvered to shore the fourteen-foot boat they had all traveled on for the last several weeks. Anya had recruited Bia to help Mac and her escape from Japanese forces closing in on them in Shanghai.

Anya and Mac stepped onto a sandy white beach as the aircraft tilted its wings, dropped its altitude, and then bore down on them. Anya focused her attention on the cockpit. Even though it was a distance, she imagined there was murderous rage in the pilot's coal-black crazy eyes. She believed it was Sun Temujin. The evil man they had left for dead back in Shanghai. She shot a glance at Mac. "I don't believe he sees fishermen."

"Everyone, run for the trees," Mac yelled.

Bia and her husband leaped out of the sampan onto shore. Anya stood immobile, fixated on the plane. Mac grabbed her hand and pulled her as he hustled for cover.

The spit of the engine turned into a steady loud buzz. Gunfire exploded from a machine gun. Bullets ricocheted off driftwood and pelted the sand. Mac dove into the tall scrub taking Anya with him. She winced from the sting of thorns that scraped her skin.

"Keep your head down," he said.

Anya curled herself into a tight ball. Her heart hammered against her chest, which forced her to breathe through her mouth. A pungent bitter scent filled her nostrils and lingered on her tongue.

Gunfire consumed the area. A loud moan rose a few feet from Anya. "Bia," Anya shouted. "Are you all right?" She popped up to search for her friend.

Mac lurched and pushed her down, but before he could reach her, three bullets hit him in the chest. His body jerked forward then back and then fell to the ground.

"Oh God—Mac." Anya rushed to his side. Her hand trembled as she placed her fingers against his neck. There was no sign of a pulse.

The enemy aircraft circled back and fired again. The force of a slug ripped into her upper arm and caused her to spin around. Two more bullets hit her, one in the thigh the other at the small of her back. She watched the plane advance again and fought to stand but the loss of leg movement held her down. *I must survive.* Tears trickled down her cheeks. "God, please let me live."

"Anya, Anya."

She felt pressure on her arm and heard a familiar voice. "Wake up. You're having a nightmare."

Anya wiped the moisture from her face and tilted her eyes away from the morning sunlight. She looked around unsure of her whereabouts. Mac knelt beside her, Bia behind him. "You're all dead."

"Not yet, sister," Mac said. "But if we don't get a move on, your dream may become a reality."

"Where are we?" Anya said.

"This is the end of our journey on water," Bia said. "The rest of the way is an arduous mountainous trek." She pointed in the distance to a stunning, jagged snow-capped mountain range.

Anya's gaze followed a dirt footpath yards from the shoreline that disappeared into a sparse grove of trees and thick khaki scrub brush choked with weeds. She stroked the snakehead pendant hung around her neck. The message inside needed to reach Edmund Atwater, her boss at the U.S. War Department in San Francisco. All hopes rested with Bia and her Communist friends to help Mac and her escape.

The men hid the sampan amid the cattails, then added tree branches on top of the canvas canopy to disguise it from air surveillance. Bia and Anya prepared supply packs of food for each to carry.

Mac hobbled towards Anya. "It's your leg again," she said. "You've been favoring it since we left Shanghai. I wish you'd let me take a look at it."

"I'm fine. It's just a wicked bruise."

"There's a village a few miles ahead where we can spend the night and find a meal," Bia said.

"Do you think they may have a way for me to transmit a message?" Anya said.

"Doubtful," Bia said. "We need to get you to a city and find someone who has the right equipment."

Mac interrupted. "Where's Nanjing from here?"

"Is this in regards to Dai Li?" Anya sighed. "Commander Benson, you need to forget it and work to get back to the States."

Mac fired back a glare that would melt an ice cube. "OSS sent me to assassinate Dai Li, the head of the Nationalist's security. My mission is over when I say it's over."

Anya's cheeks burned and she recoiled. She had believed they had put their differences to rest.

Bia ignored their quarrel and led the way single file along the path. Mac brought up the rear.

Anya ducked under a low-hanging tree branch. Not being observant the branch smacked Mac in the face. "Damn it, Anya. Don't you know anything about hiking courtesy?"

Bia twirled around and Anya gave her a broad smile.

They continued along the trail bordered by dark evergreens and giant leafless oaks stripped by winter's rage. A sweet musty aroma from damp bark permeated the air.

The sound of an airplane engine interrupted the bird songs and cricket chirps. Everyone scrambled for cover. Anya dug her fingers into the soil and pressed her body flat against the ground. *It's my dream.*

The aircraft dipped one wing and sprayed a barrage of bullets in their direction. The trees swayed which caused rotted black acorns to pelt them. Something struck Anya's thigh and she screamed.

Mac crawled to her. "Are you okay?"

"I thought I'd been shot, but I'm good."

Mac popped up and shouted, "Everyone okay?"

Anya shoved his head into the dirt. "Keep your head down."

He stood. A clump of soil clung to his cheek. "Thanks, but the plane is not circling back." He wiped his cheek.

Red faced, she said, "At least in this version we aren't riddled with bullets."

"Anya, you must be clairvoyant," Bia said.

Anya dusted herself off. "In my dream we all died."

Everyone released a hesitant chuckle except Bia's husband who spat on the ground then pumped his fist at the distant aircraft.

Bia said, "He's angry. The Japanese bombed his village with plague-infested fleas. Many of his family and friends died." She patted his shoulder and tried to calm him.

Steps ahead, the tree-lined path opened to a meadow. Wild flowers peeked above a lush carpet of green grasses. A breeze caught their floral scent from a fresh rain. Above the horizon, a gray mist shrouded the mountain range. A brisk breeze swept across Anya's cheeks. She bit her lower lip and stroked her ring. She sensed things were amiss.

Mac sidled next to Anya. "Your nightmares and the way you continually rub your finger makes me think you are dwelling on your parents."

Anya had gained a semblance of confidence with the truth about her parents' death. How Sun had murdered them and stolen the ring, but the recovery of it still seemed to trouble her. She studied the ring. The red diamond glistened in the sunlight. Anya recalled the time when her father had surprised her with it on her sixteenth birthday. She slipped it off her finger and placed it in her brassiere. "It will be safer there."

"It might help to talk." He placed a gentle hand on her shoulder.

She focused on Mac's blue eyes and caught her reflection. "It's not about my parents. It's something else. I can't explain it. It's a feeling of dread or unfinished business. I can't seem to shake it off."

"Once you get to Yan'an, the Communists' stronghold, you'll be safe," he said.

"What do you mean? Aren't you coming along?" He failed to respond, which caused her concern.

"I know you don't want to think about it, but from all you've told me I know your daughter misses you very much. I still miss my father to this day."

No response.

Anya persisted. "Her first crush will be her father. You don't want to miss that, do you?"

No response again. His eyebrows became one and his face flushed with rage. She knew she had ignited a major nerve.

MILES LATER, THEY APPROACHED a stark village where even trains failed to pass. The ramshackle buildings were set far apart from one another like a desolate town in a western movie. A rotting wooden wheelbarrow missing one wheel rested catawampus against a shack. Across the way remnants of a shop appeared on the verge of collapse. Groomed graves with white crosses stood next to a steepled church at the far end of town.

"It's an old mining town converted by English missionaries that was abolished by either the Boxer Rebellion or Japanese or Communists," Bia said. "Most headed for Burma, although I hear things aren't so good in that part of the world either."

Bia approached one of the villagers, a toothless man whose wrinkled face had seen a hard life. She asked him where they might find shelter and food. His boney finger pointed to the church. "He says it's abandoned." Bia addressed the group. "Other travelers are staying there, but we are welcome to join them. He'll have his wife bring us something to eat." Bia bowed and thanked the toothless man.

A hare jumped out from behind a barrel and darted across the road. Bia let out a surprised laugh. "It's good fortune to have a rabbit cross your path."

"We could use some," Mac said.

Anya noticed a person emerge from the church. She shaded her eyes from the setting sun to get a better look. Her brow furrowed and she sucked in a breath of air at the familiar figure.

TWO
Central China

THE SILHOUETTE OF A FIGURE LAY IN THEIR SIGHT. The group ambled along the pebbled path that led to the church. Mac trailed behind, favoring his leg. He had not yet caught a glimpse of the recognizable figure a few steps ahead. Anya rubbed her eyes in disbelief at the sight in front of her.

In the doorway, stood a young Chinese man dressed in steel blue cotton pants and tunic. He wore wire-rimmed glasses and a smile that stretched across both cheeks. Anya knew him straight away.

"Miss Anya. Mister Mac. It's good to see you again, my friends." He advanced with outstretched arms.

"Joe," Anya said. "I almost didn't recognize you without your red pullover sweater and book."

His smile retreated and he let his arms fall to his

side. The once innocent sparkle in his eyes had faded. "I left the Hardy Boys behind after Mr. Shelley's death."

"What are you doing here?" she said.

Mac spun around. Mad dog rage radiated from his face. He refused to forgive Joe for turning them over to the Green Gang—the Mafia of Shanghai. Anya had escaped. Mac almost died from the brutality at the hands of a mercenary. The image of Mac's unconscious, naked body that hung from the rafters of the deserted warehouse remained fresh in her mind. Sun Temujin had tortured him in ways that were unforgivable, but Mac never relented. Sun had not only murdered her parents and tortured Mac, had he also murdered her lover, Guy with whom she had recently reunited while on assignment in Shanghai. Sun had gunned him down during Mac's rescue. The witness of Sun's tormented death—a bullet to the gut—gave her satisfaction.

Mac clenched his hands into fists. Joe neared and Mac picked him up by his shirt collar far enough off the ground that his feet dangled. "Why I oughta… Do you know what that man did to me?" The edge of Joe's shirt cut across his larynx. Gurgles escaped his lips.

Bia and her husband stood uneasy, wide-eyed. It was their first glimpse of Mac's wrath. The entire trip upriver they had not encountered this side of him.

Anya explained Mac's ordeal and that his anger was warranted.

"Mac. Stop." Anya rushed to his side and pushed down on his arms. She smelled the musk of Joe's fear. Mac released a frightened Joe, who slumped to the ground. Anya sandwiched herself between the two and waited for Mac's eyes to meet hers before she continued. "Joe had little choice."

He glared at her then pointed to Joe and howled, "Traitor."

Joe picked himself off the ground and brushed the dirt from his backside. An elderly, hunchbacked man with a long black-and-white peppered queue shuffled towards them as though he carried a heavy weight. He muttered something to Joe.

"It's…" Joe coughed then cleared his throat. "It's nothing, Uncle." He pushed his eyeglasses against the bridge of his nose. "Go back inside."

Mac stepped forward. Joe raised his arms and stepped back. Anya blocked Mac. "See that old man?" She placed the flat of her hand against his chest. "Don't you recognize him? It's Joe's uncle. You met him weeks ago." Mac's face grimaced. "The Green Gang threatened to kill his uncle if he didn't cooperate."

"Bullshit." Mac's eyes remained riveted on Joe's movements.

"How do you think I found you in the

warehouse?" Anya said. "Joe told me where you were. He tried to redeem himself." Mac relaxed and she removed her hand. He kicked the dirt, shoved his hands into his trousers pockets, and turned away. The scowl on Mac's face told her this quarrel was not finished.

"Let's everyone go inside, Bia said. "The sun has set and I, for one, am chilled and worn-out."

Anya said, "Isn't that a good idea, Mac? Let's go in and get warm."

"I'm going for a walk. Back in a bit."

Anya watched Mac stomp away. A familiar act, but she believed he would return. She cleaned a bit of dust the wind had blown into her eye and sighed. She had grown weary of dusty roads and suitcase travel. She longed to take a hot bath. It had been weeks since she had last had a good soak or a shot of vodka.

"Is he all right?" Bia said.

"Give him time and he'll be as right as you or me."

"I thought I saw a connection between the two of you on the trip up the river," Bia said.

Anya crinkled her nose. "I respect Mac. As a naval officer, he holds honor and duty above all else. My father was a military man, he held the same principles. Besides, Mac's not my type…too pretty. And he's married. I would never cross that line."

They made their way to the church with Joe in the lead. She whispered to Bia. "I don't trust Joe either, but I am willing to give him the benefit of the doubt until he proves otherwise."

They followed Joe into the modest church. The open room looked to have held about fifty worshipers. A shadow outline was all that remained of the cross that once hung over an absent altar. A smidgen of light peeked through the dirt and grime that caked the windows. The one piece of furniture that remained was a single pew at the front.

Joe spoke in Mandarin. "The villagers have been using any wood available to keep themselves warm during the cool winter evenings. Given how little they possess, they've been most generous in sharing what they do have."

"They probably still hold onto Christian values even though they are forbidden to worship," Bia said. "Not all communities are charitable to strangers, especially to Occidentals."

Joe approached Anya with his head bowed. "I can't forgive myself for my betrayal of you both. My dreams haunt me."

"I know." She patted his back. "Family comes first."

"I don't think Mac understood the gravity of my situation. The Green Gang threatened our lives. They rule Shanghai with an iron fist, much like

Capone ran Chicago." Joe sighed. "Do you think he'll be able to look at me without teeming hatred?"

"Mac is like a racehorse with blinders. It's a skewed perspective where everyone he encounters is the enemy. His narrow viewpoint of women forced me to withhold my temper on several occasions. However, he did come around to acknowledge my contributions." A gentle smile crossed her lips. "Mac will eventually see his way to putting it all behind." They stood side-by-side in silence. *I hope.*

Two village women toddled into the room. Puffs of dust followed them as their tattered hems brushed across the stone floor. One woman carried blankets; the other had a black rice-filled pot and bowls. Bia bowed as she accepted the food and chopsticks. The women shuffled out, leaving their nervous giggles to echo throughout the hall.

Bia served each person a bowl of hot rice. The uncle as the elder received his meal before the others, according to tradition. Anya and Bia would be served last.

"I saved enough for Mac. It will be cold if he doesn't return soon," Bia said.

"He will be hungry and won't mind," Anya said. She walked to the door, stared into the darkness, and ate her rice. *I wonder where he's gone? Most likely stewing over Joe. I hope he's not thinking about Dai Li.*

"How are you holding up?" Bia said.

"I feel like Dorothy. I just want to go home, but I don't have magical red shoes."

The lines in Bia's forehead deepened and she tilted her head.

"Sorry, it's a reference to an American movie."

"Where's home?"

Anya shrugged. "I use to know but now it's uncertain." She hugged her friend. "I am glad we were able to reconnect after so long. When I left Shanghai those many years ago, I assumed I'd never return." Anya shook her head. "And here I am—back in China."

"Painful memories," Bia said.

Anya nodded. "Let's get some sleep."

They each grabbed a blanket. Hay provided added comfort against the cold floor. Uncle took the pew.

Anya curled her legs to her chest for added warmth. Once again, her thoughts wandered to Mac. *It would be like him to refuse to come inside because of Joe. The obstinate jackass.*

Bia whispered to Anya. "I'm sorry about your parents. Sun has gone to meet his ancestors. They will give him a good beating."

"I've put it behind me," she lied. Sun filled her dreams. A shiver ran through her from either the cold or her nightmares. She feared it was the latter.

THREE
Mac

MAC STORMED AWAY FROM ANYA AND THE others as they entered the church. The desolate village gave him solace as he kicked pebbles like a frustrated child. He mumbled to himself, "What in the hell am I doing here?" He raked his fingers through his thick chestnut hair. His mission had not gone as planned and he would not be content until it had been completed. His OSS future was on the line. No desk job would satisfy his hunger for adventure. He had to make things right.

The sun had set and moonlight was his one source of light. Candlelight flicked behind covered windows of shanty homes. The dirt roads were barren of people and animals. The only sounds were the buzz of flying insects and the scuttle of six-legged bugs.

Mac stopped in front of a closed shop, sank on the stoop, and massaged his leg. "I can't return home. Not now." He focused on the church and mulled long and hard about Anya. He concluded that she would be safe with Bia. She would see that Anya got home safe.

A shadow approached him. His reverent voice was familiar. He held a blanket in his hands.

THE SUN RADIATED OVERHEAD the next day as Mac trudged across the sandy beach to the sampan hidden in the cattails. The long trek had made his leg ache. He reminded himself he was a Navy man and pushed the pain out of his mind.

Mac's midsection growled. *God, what I would do for a slab of bacon and a stack of hotcakes.* He looked around the boat for something to eat. Juice from the first bite of a forgotten apple ran down his chin. He wiped the dribble with the back of his hand then continued to gobble the fruit. He rummaged for more food without luck. His stomach continued to churn.

He had a German Mauser pistol Anya had given him. What he needed was a shotgun to hunt game. *I wonder if I could catch a steelhead or a perch?* He broke off a sturdy branch from a nearby tree and honed the end on a large stone until it came to a sharp point.

Mac rolled his trouser legs up to his thighs,

waded into the river, and stood motionless. He suppressed his discomfort from the frigid temperature. Something nibbled at his ankle. He plunged the spear into the water only to miss a fish but almost took off a toe.

He waited for the water to calm and lowered the spear to just above the surface. A reflective flicker caught his eye and he thrust the spear again and pulled out a small translucent fish. It flailed for its freedom. Mac grabbed it tight as it tried to wiggle free and slapped the fish's head on the rock. He elected not to cook his catch to save time. Mac pried a piece of raw meat from the skin, hesitated, sniffed it, and then took a bite. Its texture was similar to a half-cooked potato.

Mac gorged himself on five more fish before setting out. He pushed the sampan into the river and jumped in. "Son-of-a-bitch." He had managed to hit the sore spot on his thigh. He staggered over with a moan and grabbed the long sculling oar. He maneuvered up-river and hugged the shoreline the way Bia's husband had shown him.

The water's edge evolved to rugged moss-covered cliffs the size of skyscrapers on both sides. Only the sturdiest of trees grew between the cracks. Mac passed through the narrow canyon to where the river widened. The topography changed. An open field of low growing shrubs and tall evergreens dotted the natural landscape.

An outboard approached and puttered past within a few feet. Three sets of black beady eyes had their sights on him. His neck hairs bristled. He placed a newspaper over the gun next to him. *I should have waited until after sunset before leaving shore.* He did not divert his eyes until they had rounded the bend.

Mac continued to paddle until he heard the roar of a boat motor. Japanese patrol. *Those dirty bastards must have ratted me out.* He scanned around for a place to hide. The riverbank was barren—not even a reed to use for cover.

Mac's heart raced. His palms became clammy as the Japanese closed in on him. The tip of the patrol boat came into view. Mac slid overboard into the icy river. *Shit!* He had forgotten to grab his Mauser. Positioned between land and the sampan, he hoped the soldiers would think it discarded.

The engine roared closer then the throttle eased. The wake from the powerboat made his body bob. He grabbed onto a part of the hull to maintain his position. The severe cold caused him to shiver, though his bruised leg no longer ached.

The boat tipped and he heard the clomp of a soldier onboard. A man's voice yelled out in Japanese as he approached the edge of the boat. Mac submerged. Their wake had stirred up the bottom silt and made the surface murky. He made out a silhouette that peered over the edge. Small bubbles escaped from his mouth. The silhouette hovered overhead. Mac became lightheaded. A burning sensation filled his lungs. He would have to surface soon. It came down to surrender or drown. He began to submerge when the shadow disappeared.

The boat tipped again and the engines revved. Mac reached the surface and gasped several breaths. Thankful to have escaped, he was equally glad they had left the boat intact.

Mac had scarcely finished that thought when the sound of a gun exploded. Bullets riddled the sampan's deck and pierced the hull. Mac dove to the bottom. From his expertise in firearms, he knew the sound came from the Mauser. He not only lost his means of transportation, he also lost his weapon. His head barely above the surface, Mac watched the Japanese maneuver back downstream as the sampan sank.

Mac trembled from the chill as he crawled onto shore. He collapsed spread-eagle and allowed the sun to warm him. Feeling returned to his body and his leg began to throb. It was late afternoon and night would soon be upon him. Exhausted, he pulled himself off the ground and followed a narrow path that paralleled the river.

Mac passed a small thicket of trees and heard shouts of laughter resonating beyond. *It might be a*

Japanese or Communist camp. Hopefully, a village with supplies. He crept through the trees then stopped shy of a clearing.

Ahead lay two single-level, wooden structures and a third building with a steep-pitched pagoda style roof. A stream of children hauled large white bundles into a cart. Younger ones romped and teased two over-sized donkeys the size of a mule in a corral. The children wore white shirts and short-legged black overalls, reminiscent of a parochial uniform. The black-haired girls wore their hair in two braids. Someone had used a bowl to square-off the boy's hair, which caused cowlicks to poke out in all directions.

A slender blonde-haired woman emerged from one of the smaller structures. The sun's rays outlined the shape of her silhouette behind a thin cotton dress. Her flaxen hair glistened in the twilight. Mac's heart skipped a beat and an uncontrollable throb pulsed through his groin.

The children dropped their belongings and ran to the slender woman who looked not much older than those who surrounded her. *What's she doing with all of them?* Mac hobbled towards them in silence as the children buried their faces in the skirt of her dress.

"How can we help you, sir?" The tenor of her voice was as crisp as the air. Mac imagined this siren with her alabaster skin could lure a man to his demise, a beauty best to keep at arm's length.

A thin man stepped out from the doorway. "Greetings, friend." He extended his boney-fingered hand to Mac. The gaunt man, his face the color of paste, stood several inches shorter than Mac. His shirt hung from him as though still on a wire hanger, which gave him the appearance of a scarecrow. "I'm Mathew and this here is Scarlet. What can we do for you?"

He heard an accent of either South African or Aussie. He never could distinguish between the two. "The name's Mac Benson." They exchanged handshakes. "I am making my way to Chungking and in need of a meal and a sleep."

"I think we can help you." He turned to Scarlet. "What do you say, Mother?" She returned his glance and nodded.

"I notice you have a limp. My wife can tend to your leg."

Mac's eyes darted to Scarlet then back to Mathew who looked twice her age. Mac held in a smile. "Thanks. It's nothing."

"We are missionaries in search of a safe haven for these Christian orphans," Mathew said. Mac noticed for the first time that all the children were Chinese. A boy looked up at Mac with a toothless grin.

"We plan to leave at sunrise before the soldiers come to murder us and take our animals for food. You're welcome to join us. We're also heading west. We'll camp along the way and find shelter where available," he said.

Mac glanced into Scarlet's amber brown eyes. She stared doe-eyed at him then gently took him by the arm, above the elbow, and escorted him inside.

"Let's take a look at that leg," she said.

FOUR
Anya

ANYA WOKE TO THE RATTLE OF TEACUPS. SHE stretched and yawned and pulled herself off the mashed down hay. "Ouch." A sharp pain ran through her neck. She grabbed the muscle and tried to massage out the kink. A night on a cold stone floor had been too much for her bones.

Joe handed her a small bowl. "Uncle packed his special teas. This blend will give you energy for the long journey ahead."

Anya blew on the hot aromatic liquid then took a sip. Jasmine, ginger, and clove permeated her sinuses. "It's excellent." She bowed to Uncle, sipped her tea, then wandered outside. Anya returned and stood in the church doorway. "Has anyone seen Mac?"

"He didn't come in all night. Let me ask around

the village," Bia said.

Joe slinked up to Anya. "I gave Mr. Mac a blanket to make peace last night. But he only wanted information about Dai Li." He lowered his eyes. "I told him that before Uncle and I left Shanghai, we heard rumors that Du Yu-seng deserted his Green Gang and fled to Hong Kong. And Li headed for Chungking to meet General Chiang Kai-shek."

Anya pursed her lips.

"Did I do something wrong?" Joe raised his eyebrows.

"No. It's just…it's nothing," Anya said. She rested against the door jam. *Why would Mac believe Joe? Had he finally forgiven him, or was it desperation to believe anything about Li?*

Bia returned with a frown. "A villager says he saw a big man walk out of town at sunrise."

Anya sighed. "He's gone to Chungking."

"Does he know how to get there?"

"He'll find a way." Anya downed the final sip of tea and placed the bowl on a barrel next to her. "He's on a mission and won't quit until it's completed. I can't help him. I must get back to the States." She grasped the pendant that hung from her neck. "I need to transmit a message."

Joe piped in. "I can help you, Anya."

"How?"

He adjusted his wire-rimmed glasses against the

bridge of his nose. "You forget, I worked as Sheldon Henderson's assistant at the American Consulate in Shanghai. I know every attaché in China. I can take you to Shinjing. It's a good day's journey south. There we'll find a contact to help us."

"I don't know." Anya was still skeptical of Joe, but she remembered what Mac had told her. 'At some point you have to trust someone or you'll never accomplish your mission.' She wrung her hands. "I'm sure it's overrun with Japanese."

"It may be your only option if you wish to reach your superior," Bia said.

"What about Uncle?" Anya said.

"We can take him north to a stronghold. He will be safe with us," Bia said. "You can use the sampan."

"It's settled. We start for Shinjing," Joe said.

Anya pressed her fingers against her temples and exhaled. "I'll need a good disguise."

ANYA'S MIND WANDERED BACK to Shanghai as she and Joe made their way back to the river. *All Mac and I had gone through together and he up and leaves without a word. What a rotter.*

The warmth of the afternoon sun beat down on them. Anya plucked a long weed from the side of the path and twisted it around her finger.

The long walk gave Anya an opportunity to pry into Joe's personal life. Before she put her life entirely into his hands, she wanted to know a little more about him. "How did you fall into the hands of missionaries?"

Joe was forthcoming. "The Boxers killed my family before I could walk. I don't remember them or how I ended up in the hands of the English. They said I was curled up in a box starving to death when they found me.

"They were a funny people—kind yet strict. They tried to indoctrinate their Christian values on me." He shrugged. "It didn't take. They used a ruler on my knuckles if I failed to recite the week's verses. It still didn't work.

"Rural farm life is simple and hard. I never had anything of my own, always hand-me-down clothes and shoes. Meals were a pale gray gruel without meat for weeks at a time. I could hardly wait until I was old enough to leave. It's not that I blame them. They did the best they knew how. I wanted more, so I went in search of an uncle they told me who lived in Shanghai."

"What led you to become so enamored with the Hardy Boys books?"

"I worked at the Canidrome, a dog track, very chichi. My duties were mainly waiter and dishwasher. Mister Shelley frequented the place. He took a shine to me. One day gave me a book he said I'd enjoy. It was the Hardy Boys *The Tower Treasure*. We would chat about the boys' escapades. I enjoyed our time together. He regarded me as a friend rather than a coolie, like the others.

"I identified more with the younger Hardy brother, Joe. He was close to my age and I wanted to be just like him. He was witty and good-humored. He would dash into a situation without consequences and come out looking good. To dress in all manner of disguises and solve mysterious crimes. To chase criminals on a motorcycle and unravel complex clues. To be the hero." Joe laughed. "I was so captivated by it all that I changed my name to Joe." He paused and gazed into the distance. "I miss those carefree days.

"What do you miss?"

Anya laughed and paused. "I miss the complex scent of French perfume that makes men turn their heads. The elegance of a chiffon and velvet-laced ball gown against my skin. Handsome men in tails and top hats, and of course, military uniforms. I miss the accompaniment of an orchestra playing a Strauss waltz. Russian caviar, vodka, and mostly Borman chocolates."

"Do you think the world will ever be at peace?" Joe said.

"I pray so."

They arrived at the river's edge to discover the sampan gone. "Mac's got it," Anya said.

"It doesn't matter," Joe said. "Our destination is on the other side of the river. There's a village several hours from here where we can get supplies and a change of clothes.

"How do you plan we get across?"

"Swim."

Before Anya could protest, Joe pushed her into the brush.

"What the hell," she cried.

He put his finger to his lips and whispered. "It's a Japanese patrol boat."

Anya peered through the bushes. Her body trembled as the boat neared. It coasted near the shoreline, close enough that Anya saw a gun pointed at Joe. A piece from the wooden grip was missing. She sucked in air to calm her heartbeat. It was Mac's Mauser. *Oh my God. They've killed Mac.* An ache in her chest pulsated.

Anya flinched at the sound of gunfire. A couple of bullets struck at Joe's feet. Sand flew up and landed on his pants legs. He remained frozen like a rabbit when a predator is near.

A soldier called out to him in Mandarin, "What are you doing here?"

Joe bowed. "I am on my way to visit a friend and stopped by the river for a drink of water."

The soldiers chuckled to one another, studied him for a second, then resumed down river. Joe remained bent over until they were out of sight, then walked over to Anya and helped her out of the brambles.

"That was Mac's gun," Anya said. "I fear he's dead or worse, a prisoner."

"They wouldn't have harassed me if they had a prisoner. Mac is very resourceful. I'll bet he abandoned the sampan and headed out on foot. If he's alive and follows this river west, it will lead into the great Chang Jiang River, what you English call the Yangtze. It leads straight into Chunking."

Anya turned and focused upstream. "I hope he's okay."

"He's in Buddha's hands now," Joe said.

THE SWIM ACROSS THE RIVER had left their clothes heavy with silt. A rutted dirt road led them into a small town. Along an alley, they found laundry twisting in the wind. Since they had no money, necessity forced them to steal what they needed.

In unison, they dashed to the clothesline and each snatched a top and pants. A small woman sprinted out from the house. A wooden spoon flailed overhead. In his escape, Joe ran into a large sheet and got tangled up in it. The small woman hit him with her spoon, another whap to his back and a wallop on his keister. He pulled the cloth off the line and fought to unravel it from between his legs while she beat him. He managed to untangle himself.

Anya yelled, "This way, Joe."

He raced to her. They both took off as the small woman screamed obscenities at them. They were far from town before they stopped running.

"Are you all right?" Anya said.

"That…" He caught his breath. "That was a crazy woman. She tried to kill me."

Anya snickered. "Headlines—read all about it. Man killed by wooden spoon."

THEY ARRIVED IN SHINJING the next day. Anya used a conical bamboo hat she had pilfered from a street cart. Its wide brim helped to hide her occidental face.

Shinjing was similar to Shanghai. Its European gothic structures mixed with an Eastern flair. To Anya, Shinjing lacked the electricity that made Shanghai mystic and alluring. It did not yield bright colors; its hue resembled industrial drab. There were fewer buses, fewer streetcars, fewer automobiles, but hordes of rickshaws and bicycles. The people had a peasant appearance as they shuffled along the streets in black cotton shoes and floor length, plain robes. A handful dressed in western attire. She inhaled. The air held a pleasant earthy quality, unlike Shanghai's rancid stench.

"I know where we might locate someone to help us," Joe said.

Anya lowered her head and followed Joe. He walked into a noodle shop and headed for the back. They passed several men seated at tables. She discerned from their leather shoes they were businessmen. One man moved his patent leather shoe from under the table, but she was able to avoid tripping over it. She wondered if he did it to try to get her to look up.

"Stay here for a moment," Joe said. He left her in the empty room and returned to the front.

Anya fidgeted. She pondered about the last time Joe said those words just before he handed her over to the Green Gang. *There comes a time when you have to trust someone.* Anya swallowed hard and tried to quell her fears.

Footsteps approached as she looked for an escape, then a weapon. The curtain door fluttered and her heart raced. It was Joe. Behind him stood a tall, slender Chinese man dressed in a well-tailored suit. Joe lowered his voice. "This is a friend. He works with people who can get you what you need."

"I'm Longfu." He extended his hand, western style, but spoke in Mandarin.

Anya relaxed, removed her hat, and gave him a Mona Lisa smile. She wiped her moist palm on her pants leg, then shook his hand. "Nice to meet you."

Longfu directed himself to Joe. "Where are you staying?"

"I know of a hotel in the Hankou district."

Longfu clacked his tongue. "That place was bombed out years ago. I will take you to my sister's home. It's not fancy, but it offers a warm meal and a bed."

At that instant, Anya craved a bath and a hot meal more than sleep. And she would have killed for a shot of vodka.

FIVE
Anya

A RAY OF SUNLIGHT FROM A SMALL PORTAL LIKE window flickered across Anya's face. She opened one eye then the other and threw the covers over her head. The scuffle of feet across the wood floor outside her room caused her to toss the covers aside. She sat at the edge of her cot and stretched her legs until they touched the wall of her closet-sized room. Her sleep was restful, void of nightmares. A blessing, she thought.

Someone knocked at the paper-thin door. "Are you ready? Joe said. "We should get going."

"Yes, putting on my shoes. I'll be there in a few minutes." She put on her black slipper-shoes. She wore a black Chinese tunic and pants borrowed from Longfu's sister. She pinned her hair back, grabbed her stolen hat, and headed downstairs. She found Joe and Longfu sitting, drinking tea.

"Good morning." Anya joined the men. Longfu's sister said nothing as she served tea, then quietly left. Anya watched her glide out of the room. She had an elegance about her that Anya admired. "What's the plan, gentlemen?"

Longfu said, "As I explained to Joe, when the Japanese interned all Westerners, one of the first places they raided were the foreign nationalist government buildings. Washington had warned us days earlier that things were going to heat up. We'd been ordered to destroy all documents and electronic equipment. Before we could get the Americans out, the Japanese stormed the compound."

"Where are they detained?" Anya said.

"The Japanese have converted several buildings and hotels into prisons to prevent American bombing raids on the city," Longfu said. "A few of us managed to snatch the telegraph key and wiring, any communication equipment. We stuffed things down our trousers. They didn't bother to search any Chinese. They think we are stupid and work with the Americans for money. They do not believe we possess loyalty to anyone but ourselves."

Anya placed her hand on Longfu's forearm. "Thank you for your help. And you, too, Joe. I don't know what I would do without you both. Do you still have the equipment?"

Longfu nodded. "We've set it up in an abandoned building that got bombed during the '37 Japanese raids. We transmit enemy movement to our contact in Honolulu. We avoid relaying much of any value to the Nationalists. We don't trust them anymore than the Communists."

"What are we waiting for? Let's go," Anya said.

She walked behind Joe and Longfu with her head held low. They wove through the crowds without incident. At one point, they passed two Japanese soldiers. Anya shuffled along and prayed they would ignore her. The soldiers marched passed without question. She let out a quiet sigh satisfied her disguise had succeeded.

They walked across vacant lots and rail tracks until they reached a burned-out warehouse on the edge of town. Most of the windows no longer held glass, daylight pierced through holes in the exterior walls where once mortar held bricks. They continued along the fallen rubble and descended three floors to a broad corridor. Dripping pipes extended for several meters along the ceiling. They sloshed along the wet floor. The musty odor reminded her of the underground tunnels in Shanghai. Muffled sounds grew more distinct then voices emerged as they reached the end of the hall.

They walked into a room filled with artificial light. Exposed blubs and wiring hung from the ceiling and walls. Laid out on a large table was a city map. A group of Chinese men and women looked up.

"We have guests." Longfu extended his arm in a sweeping motion. "These are the men and women of the Shinjing resistance."

Mumbles and whispers swelled. One man approached while the others resumed their business. He was short, not much taller than Anya. His rolled-up sleeves exposed a coin-sized tattoo on his forearm. Anya recognized the Chinese characters and their meaning of freedom. She noticed his bruised knuckles when he rolled down his sleeves.

"Why have you brought them here?" The man's arms flailed.

"Calm down, Wushi." Longfu laid a hand on his shoulder. "They have asked for our help."

Wushi pulled away. "You bring strangers to our best hideout. Are you insane?"

Joe shifted his weight and glanced over at Anya.

"This woman is an American working with their secret service." Longfu said. "They are both trustworthy."

"How can she be trusted? She's not even Chinese."

"I understand your concern." Anya stepped forward.

Wushi stammered. "You know…Mandarin?"

"I lived in Shanghai for many years before the war as an exiled Russian. You can believe what Longfu tells you."

Wushi scowled and crossed his arms at his chest.

Anya addressed Longfu. "I must use your equipment."

"Okay, but it must be short so the enemy can't detect the signal location." He led her to a table with a radio transmitter and telegraph key. She placed the earphones over her head, flipped the metal switch on, rotated the dial to the correct frequency, and then tapped out her message for Edmund Atwater.

```
Officer missing.
Need transportation home.
```

"It might be days before we hear back," Longfu said.

"Maybe there is something I can do to assist your group," she said.

"Such as?"

"I'm pretty good with a pistol and I speak Japanese."

Longfu rubbed his chin. "We have a visitor," he chuckled, "who may have vital information. He has been uncooperative."

"I'm a translator, not a torturer," Anya said.

ANYA STOOD IN THE HALLWAY and waited for

Longfu to return. A loud bang stole her attention and she went to investigate. She found Wushi hunched over, tinkering with a metal pipe. She decided this might be a good time to make amends rather than worry about a knife thrown in her direction later. She understood his disdain for foreigners, the fear of losing their culture. She wiped her nose on a hanky. "I think I'm coming down with a cold."

"It's the mold. Everyone here has a runny nose," he said without looking up. He continued to fiddle. "Can you get something for me?"

"I guess."

"In the next room, on the table is a small vial, like a tube. Can you bring it to me?"

She entered the area filled with all manner of powders and liquids. Scattered about were beakers and glass tubes. On a small table next to a burner was a wire rack that held several small compartments. One of the compartments housed a vial that contained a colorless liquid.

The sound of thunder from outside echoed throughout the room. Anya stretched her arm to pick up the vial when the crash of a lightning bolt struck nearby and made her blink and jump back. She regained her composure and went for the object again. Her hand hovered over it.

"Stop," Longfu shouted.

Anya pulled back her arm and stood frozen. Her heart raced and she placed her hands over her chest as if to slow the beat. "What?"

"This is a live explosive," Longfu said. "It's a good thing I happened to pass by and see you. If you had mishandled that in any way, you would have lost your arm or worse."

Joe entered. "What's all the yelling?"

"Oh nothing," Anya said. "I just almost blew myself up."

Longfu said, "In the future it would be best if you stayed out of here."

"Fine," she said as Longfu walked on.

Anya turned to Joe. "I need you to watch my back. I think Wushi tried to kill me."

SIX
Mac

MAC WOKE REFRESHED AND EAGER TO GET ON the road. He rubbed his bad leg and noticed the ache had subsided overnight. *Whatever Chinese voodoo Scarlet applied had worked.*

Children's voices drew his attention to where Scarlet and her husband, Matthew, had loaded them into a canvas-covered wagon hitched to the two over-sized donkeys. "We are leaving," Mathew said. "If you plan to travel with us, best get packed."

Mac had nothing except the soiled clothes he wore. "Ready."

The three adults led the way on foot while the children bounced about in the wagon. Dust from the windswept dirt road filled their nostrils. The late winter's warm sun reminded them that spring would come soon. Mac was grateful for the clanging of mule bells that eclipsed the children's quarreling voices that grew restless in their confinement. He spotted movement ahead in the brush and held up his hand for everyone to stop.

"What is it?" Mathew said.

Mac spun around and put his finger to his lips. He motioned for them to stay while he moved ahead. Branch leaves at the side of the road quivered, and a rustle in the weeds heightened his senses. A dry branch cracked, and then a pop echoed from a foot that stepped on something hard. A man wearing tattered clothes appeared onto the road. Starvation showed in his sunken cheeks.

"What can we do for you, friend?" Mathew spoke to him in Mandarin.

"I'm hungry," he replied. His hands remained in his pockets.

Mathew turned and said. "Scarlet, give the poor soul a little something to eat."

Mac approached Mathew and whispered, "Be careful, he looks as crooked as a pig's tail."

"Nonsense. He's hungry and will be on his way once he fills his belly." Mathew's face went ashen. Mac spun around, a pistol pointed at his chest.

Mathew put his hands together as if to pray. "We have nothing of value."

"You have a couple of hinny," the bandit said.

"We need them to transport the children."

"That's not my concern." He strolled over to the donkeys and began to unhitch them. Mac inched his way close to the thief, but before he could tackle him, the man turned. Mac grabbed the thief's arm so the barrel pointed up. A shot fired. The children screamed. Mac continued to struggle to get the gun. The thief twisted around, causing the barrel to point inward at his midsection. Another shot rang out and the intruder collapsed to the ground. The smell of sulfur from the gunpowder lingered in the air.

The children wailed as Mac picked up the pistol and examined it. It was a Japanese Nambu. He checked the magazine. Three bullets remained. He needed a gun. He had lost his Mauser when he jumped into the river to avoid the Japanese patrol. Mac rummaged through the dead man's pockets but found nothing. He picked up the body and tossed it into the bushes.

Mathew made a sign of the cross on the dead man's forehead and prayed.

"No time for that, Reverend. Where there's one, there may be others. Like ants at a picnic."

Mathew re-hitched the jacks while Mac removed the bells and tossed them. "Let's not warn anyone else we're coming."

Mathew nodded.

They decided to try their luck for shelter in the village ahead. On the outskirts of town, small huts dotted the landscape. They entered the town. A frail, gray-haired woman in a long black dress stood and stared at them with lifeless eyes as she puffed on a pipe.

"She's a witch," one child shouted and recoiled.

"Possessed by the devil," another said.

Scarlet grabbed the cross from around her neck and held it up. The witch stood up, extended a gnarly finger, and from deeps within her bowels let out a screech that made Mac's flesh crawl. Mathew slapped the butt of one donkey to pick up the pace.

The remote village had a few single-story stone buildings with gray tiled roofs. The tilt on one structure looked like a breeze could topple it. It was rural without a chicken, goat or pig in sight. Several villagers lined the street to inspect the foreigners. Mothers snatched barefoot children away before they got too close.

"They appear unfriendly," Mac said.

"I don't think they've seen many strangers," Mathew said.

"Could be the fact we're missionaries escorting Chinese children," Scarlet said.

"God will protect us," Mathew said.

After much bargaining and a handful of silver coins surrendered, a disgruntled Chinese man allowed them to stay in his barn. The dilapidated structure smelled of damp, rotten wood. Cold air seeped between the wallboards. Mac saw movement in a pile of matted hay.

Scarlet said, "The bugs will surely dine on us tonight."

A hunched-back woman entered the stable. She carried a pot of hot water and millet. Scarlet thanked her then poured the hot liquid over the grain. Hungry fingers dipped into the pot of tasteless gruel. The arduous journey had left Mac famished. He hesitated for a second, and then joined in.

Scarlet wiped food from the corner of her mouth with her finger then licked it. "That was very brave, what you did earlier. The bandit, I mean."

Mac smiled. "I dislike pushy people."

"I appreciate a man who can handle himself. It makes a woman feel safe to know she can count on one, when needed."

Mac felt his face flush. Mathew watched the two like a mother grizzly.

DAWN HAD ALMOST BROKEN when a young woman scarcely out of pigtails rushed into the barn and awakened everyone. "The town folk don't like strangers, especially Christians. There's talk about handing you over to the Japanese or stoning you," she said. "If you're going—go."

Mac stumbled out into the early morning darkness where he faced an irate mob with lanterns held high. There were several shouts then the crowd of twenty made their way to the stable.

Mac raced back inside. Mathew, Scarlet, and the children were knelt in prayer. "This is no time for praying, preacher. Everyone into the wagon—now."

He took a pitchfork and smashed it against the warped back barn wall. Three flimsy boards popped out. He pounded out more boards until it was wide enough for the cart to get through. The sound of the mob grew near.

He grabbed the halter from one of the donkeys and led them into the open. Mathew tried to whip them to go, but they refused to budge. Mac grabbed a stone and threw it. It landed on the hindquarters of one of the jackasses. The ass brayed and reared. Mac jumped on the rear of the cart as it took off. He turned to see the light from the villagers' lanterns fade as they sped away. Enraged voices continued to echo in the darkness.

THE SUN WAS HIGH in the sky before they believed they were safe enough to stop and rest beside a stream. Mac lay down next to the donkeys that grazed. He plucked a weed and chewed on its end. Beside the cart, Mathew held a toddler in his arms and caressed her cherub face. The other children corralled around him, as they often did whenever he was present. *He's like a piped-piper to them.* Mac smiled.

The children's resilience after witnessing a killing and then an irate mob who wanted them dead amazed him. *They've probably become accustomed to violence in their short lives.* He shook his head.

MAC SCRAPED HIS CHIN with the razor he borrowed from Mathew. He used his shirt to clean off his face. A young boy came up to him and wrapped his arms around one of his legs. Mac patted his head.

"They are grateful to have you along," Mathew said.

"They don't really know me." The child hurried off to join the others.

"They believe you're a good man. I do, too."

Mac looked into Mathews soulful eyes and wished he could agree.

"How did you come by these children?" Mac said.

"A widow who could no longer care for her child, pleaded with me to take her son. The word must have gotten out, or perhaps by instinct, we would find them on our doorstep. Many are Hunxie—mixed blood. To the Chinese it is a symbol of racial impurity—untouchables. A few of the young girls twelve and thirteen escaped the Japanese sex-slave camps. They were lured in with the promise of factory work to pay off family debt only to find out that their mothers had sold them. Others are from unwed mothers or courtesans. It's a mixed bag."

Mac's mind bent back to his three-year-old daughter. He had not allowed himself to think about his wife and little girl. An overwhelming urge to hold them tight and never let them go tugged at him. It had been weeks since he had left home, but this was war and he had a job to do.

"How long will you be with us?" Scarlet said.

Mac cast a glance into her amber eyes and gulped. *A lonely man carrying a bit of guilt can get himself into a world of trouble.*

SEVEN
Anya

ANYA AND LONGFU STOOD IN FRONT OF A wooden cage the size of a standard prison cell. Inside, a man lay on the floor in a fetal position with his back to them. Longfu raked a stick across the bars and yelled for the prisoner to stand. The man remained motionless. Longfu unlocked the door, hollered again without a response, then rolled the prisoner on his back.

Anya gasped at the Japanese man's swollen face. His discolored cheeks were puffed up to twice their normal size. His eyes were small slits. Dried blood stained his mouth and chin. He was barely coherent. She questioned Wushi's bruised knuckles and gave Longfu a somber gaze.

"If hypnosis worked, don't you think we would have used it?" Longfu said. "Don't harbor any compassion for this man. He is the enemy."

She diverted her eyes. A chill ran down her spine. The Japanese could be equally, if not more brutal, to their prisoners. She recalled Mac's unconscious body hanging from the rafters.

Longfu slapped the prisoner's cheek to bring him back to consciousness. "It's not anything we enjoy. However, it is necessary." Longfu's sleeve pushed up when he touched the prisoner. Anya noticed the mark on his arm. It was the same tattoo as on Wushi's arm. He met her stare.

"It means freedom. It gives us strength and displays our loyalties."

"I admire the symbolism but wonder if it exposes you to danger."

"It is a risk we are willing to take," he said.

The prisoner unleashed a moan. He mumbled something unrecognizable.

"He keeps saying the same thing over and over again, but we can't make it out. Maybe you can help."

Anya knelt and leaned her ear close to the man's shallow breath. "I think he's saying, tomorrow. What have you tried to beat out of him?"

"One of our men was captured a few days ago. We believe they plan to relocate him. This man is a prison guard. We believe he knows the where and when of it."

"Well," Anya said, "it sounds like it's going to go down tomorrow."

Longfu grabbed the prisoner's shirt collar and shook him. His limp torso bobbed like a ragdoll. "What time, goddamn it? What time?"

Anya laid her hands on Longfu. "Let me see if he will talk to me."

Longfu released his grip and the man slumped to the ground.

Anya sidled next to the prisoner. "Can you get me a towel and a bowl of water?"

Longfu yelled down the hallway. Within minutes, a woman appeared with a basin and a rag.

Anya dipped the cloth in the water, rung it out and wiped the man's face. She turned to Longfu "What is the name of your man?"

"Zang."

Anya whispered into the prisoner's ear "Tell me when they plan to move Zang, and they won't hurt you anymore. I promise."

The prisoner tried to open his eyes. A hint of white shone through one slit. Anya placed her ear to his lips. A gurgle escaped. "He says he doesn't know."

Longfu pushed Anya aside and backhanded the prisoner. He then clutched the man's genitals and squeezed them in his fist. The prisoner let out a squeal that echoed down the hallway. Anya covered her mouth and choked back the bile that rose in her throat.

"Okay, that's enough. Let me talk to him again." She leaned over the man. "Please tell me the plan, and they will stop."

His lips moved in silence. "I think he's praying," Anya said.

Longfu pulled a pistol from his waistband.

Anya held up her hand. "Wait. There's more. He said early morning. That's all he knows."

Longfu pointed the gun and shot the prisoner pointblank in his temple. "Come on. We need to put a rescue plan together."

Anya stared at the dead body. The cold-blooded act left her frozen and numb. Entangled with this group, she now had to keep one eye on Longfu, the other on Wushi, and a third eye on how to get home.

A COLD BREEZE RAN through the dank underground hideout. More than the frigid air caused Anya to shiver. After witnessing the murder of the prisoner, she questioned this cabal's moral fiber. *It's war, after all, but does that make it right?*

Eight partisan members stood around a city map of Shinjing that extended across a square table. Longfu positioned himself next to Anya and Joe. A few members stretched to see over others' shoulders while two tried to gain a better position and pushed each other to get closer.

Voices grew loud, Wushi's in particular. "I want

assurances that Zang's rescue will go without a hitch."

Longfu said, "There is an element of danger in any mission. No one can offer such a promise."

Anya wondered about Zang's and Wushi's relationship.

The overhead lights flickered. Everyone grew quiet. A loud rumble caused the room to shake. Anya's eyes widened. "Tanks." Longfu pointed up. "We fear one day we may find them in our laps." All eyes followed the sound as it passed overhead then faded.

Longfu continued, "Here's what our intelligence has gathered. Zang is being held here." He pointed to the Japanese stronghold location on the map. "Where they plan to move him is anyone's guess. According to our source, we believe it will be tomorrow morning."

The vision of the dead prisoner Longfu shot sprang into Anya's mind. It had only been a few hours earlier when he held his last lungful.

"So, we surround the place, and when they move him into the car we attack, right?" Wushi said.

"Not exactly," Longfu said. "We need to ambush them a distance from the compound where they have fewer forces. We can't afford to lose anyone, especially Zang." He winked at Wushi. "A good diversion should confuse them enough for us to snatch him."

"What kind of a distraction?" Anya said.

"That's where you come into play," Longfu said.

"What?" Wushi crossed his arms over his chest. Anya felt the burn of Wushi's eye on her without looking in his direction and heard him curse her under his breath.

"We need her." Longfu gave Wushi a solid glare.

Joe said, "I can do it."

"Sorry, little guy. For this job we need a woman."

Anya patted Joe's shoulder then nodded to Longfu before locking her knees to stop them from shaking. She listened intently as Longfu unfolded his plan.

ANYA SAT IN A silver two-seater French Amilcar parked along the side of the road. The street was empty. The resistance had alerted the residents to remain inside their homes and shops.

She strummed her fingers on the steering wheel and waited for instructions. She considered her future at the end of all the chaos of kidnappings and killings. *What will my place be in this world?* She clutched the steering wheel with both hands and held on tight.

Her decision to come to China, albeit somewhat forced upon her by Atwater, had been the right choice. It was in Shanghai where she discovered the truth about her parents' death and their assassin, Sun Temujin. She remembered Mac had told her she would make a good spy. She balked at the idea and laid her head on top of her hands. *What's to become of you girl?*

A loud crackle came across the Handie-Talkie radio transmitter that rested on the passenger's seat. "Anya, are you there? Over."

She pushed down on the talk button. "Yes, I'm here." She released the button. There was a lengthy pause from the other side.

"You have to say over after you're done speaking. Over."

"Oh, okay. Over." Laughter roared across the receiver before she released the button. Her face grew hot.

"The fox is approaching the junction. You're good to go. Over."

"On my way." She placed the talkie on the passenger seat then snatched it back. "Over and out."

She slammed the stick-shift into gear, maneuvered the bug-eyed vehicle to the middle of the intersection, stopped the engine, and stepped out of the car to wait. Her long black wig caused her scalp to itch. She readjusted the hairpiece then straightened the red cheongsam making sure the slit exposed one leg. The other leg concealed a Beretta secured by a garter. Her skin went tight as goose bumps formed from the cool morning air.

In the distance, the thunder of engines barreled down on her with a two-man tank in the lead. Anya tried to even her breathing as they neared. The tank slowed and rumbled to a stop a few feet from her. A large black sedan behind the tank slammed on its brakes. The smell of burnt rubber infused the air. A Japanese soldier peered out from the top of the tank. He yelled and waved for her to move.

Facing the enemy head on made her question if she could pull it off. Her orders were to stand her ground and make the motorcade stop.

A head popped out from the side window of the car and shouted. The soldier fixed his attention on Anya then back at the auto. An officer emerged from the sedan and stomped up to the tank. Anya overheard their conversation in Japanese. "Get this damn tank moving, soldier. That's an order."

The soldier pointed to Anya. The officer stared at her. "What do we have here?"

The pulse in her ears throbbed. She smiled and twirled the ends of her wig.

The officer said, "Come on down from there soldier. We'll push her car to the side."

At that moment, the tailgate of a parked cargo truck swung open and five resistance men leaped out with guns drawn. Longfu led the charge. They attacked the convoy like a tsunami. Longfu shot the officer as he stepped forward. Anya drew her gun from under her dress and shot the tank soldier before he could fire off a round. His limp body dangled across the gray vehicle. A launched grenade exploded inside the tank. The others rushed the car. They shot pointblank at the driver's window. The driver slumped over the steering wheel. The car lurched forward and crashed into the tank. Two resistance men simultaneously yanked open both of the back-seat doors.

"Zang's not here," a partisan fighters yelled at Longfu.

"What do you mean?" Longfu and Anya rushed over to find the leather seat empty.

EIGHT
Mac

The rocky road had worn through the soles of Mac's shoes. He had placed cardboard at the toe of each shoe but jagged pebbles managed to hit the same sore spot on his left foot. Another stone hit its mark. "Dang it." He tried to curtail his rhetoric for the sake of the children. It would be several days before he would reach Chungking. Suffering would be a constant.

Mac felt an arm wrap around his. Like a movie camera filming a matinee idol, Scarlet's eyes intruded on his every move. He unhooked their arms. "Hasn't anyone ever explained to you it's dangerous to toy with a man?"

She shadowed him as they trod along the potholed dirt road. Mathew lagged behind with the donkey team and children who recited Bible verses in the covered wagon.

"I read somewhere that flirtation is the sincerest form of flattery," she said.

"Imitation is the sincerest of flattery." He corrected her.

"I like my version better." She twirled a curl of her hair that hung across her cheek. "Do you find me attractive?"

Mac gave himself the time to study her. She was the kind of woman men surrendered themselves to. Her curves were in all the right places, and he was certain if he stroked her alabaster skin, it would feel like cold silk. But she was still a child in his eyes. He snickered at her taunts. "How did you end up here?"

Scarlet exhaled hard and turned her head away. "My parents, missionaries, died from the bubonic plague four years ago in Ningbo. One day everything was wonderful, then the next day thousands were dead." She wiped a fallen tear.

He was unsure if it was sincerity or for his benefit.

She continued. "The others didn't know what to do with me so they married me off to him." She pointed to Mathew. "I was fifteen. What did I know of marriage or men or life? Now I'm stuck with this man, who by the way has yet to touch me…if you know what I mean." She winked and laughed. "Are you amazed that women have thoughts about their love life."

His scalp prickled. He placed his hands in his pockets and swallowed hard. His head remained forward. He did not intend to discuss sex with a child.

"I wish for a more glamorous existence," she sighed. "The kind you read about in magazines. Lavish parties…jeweled gowns…exotic travel."

"There is a war on, you know. Not much time for skipping round the world."

"You seem the type who likes to travel." She walked her fingers up his arm.

Mac did not take her tease seriously. Nevertheless, he was anxious to crush it before it became contentious among the three of them. He was in an unfamiliar country without knowledge of the terrain and needed their help to get to Chungking. "I hear your husband calling you."

She ignored the pleas and kept on walking. Mathew's voice grew louder. She stopped and faced him. This gave Mac the opportunity to race ahead.

"Later," she yelled at Mac.

Mac shook his head at Scarlet's unabashed boldness in spite of her husband's presence. He reflected on his wife, Helen. The last words he had spoken to her were harsh and he was now sorry. It was not marriage he disliked, but it had become restrictive—a prison sentence. It was the reason he had taken the Shanghai assignment. He had to prove he was able to master a covert mission. That or face office boredom for the rest of his life. And at thirty-five, he believed he still had a lot to offer his country.

THEY STOPPED AND MADE CAMP in a secluded meadow. Mac had intentionally led them away from the road to avoid patrols or bandits. He sat on his heels and watched the children play a game of tag. One boy in particular, smaller and less agile than the others, seemed to receive more abuse—harder slaps, pushes, and shoves. Mac studied their interaction. The lad seemed to allow their torment, almost provoked it, Mac thought. He deliberately got in the path of the bigger ones. At one point, an older boy knelt behind the small fellow while another pushed him backwards.

Mac clacked his tongue. *That old trick. Boys will be boys in any culture.* The lad got up and brushed himself off while the others ran towards the sound of Scarlet's call to dinner.

The group stood in a circle and held hands, heads bowed. Mac shuffled his feet and watched as they said grace. They concluded and Mac took his plate of beans and sat next to the boy the others had picked on. The lad raised his head. Narrow almond-shaped somber black eyes gazed up at Mac. The boy's hair was in need of a proper cut and he, too, could use a new pair of shoes.

"What is your name?" Mac said.

"They call me Jacob."

"I am Mac." He shook the boy's hand who seemed stunned by Mac's gesture.

"Tell me, Jacob, why do you tolerate the other kids' punishment?"

The boy shrugged. "It's the one way they'll let me play with 'em."

Mac wanted to help Jacob. Maybe it was because his older brothers had tormented him as a youngster. "How about we finish up here, and I'll show you a way you can join in and not get beat up in the process."

The boy took on a grin that seemed to engulf his entire face, which caused beans to spurt between his lips.

"You like the beans?" Mac said.

"It's better than rats."

Mac stifled a retch before he spoke. "What do you mean?"

"Before the missionaries took me in, I had a family. We lived on a rice farm but didn't have much. My father couldn't bring himself to tell us what we'd eaten. Sometimes it was cat." Jacob shrugged.

"What happened to your parents?"

"Killed by bandits—all of them, mother, father, and sister. A bullet was stuck in my side." He lifted his shirt to show Mac his scar. "They left me for dead, but the missionaries found me, healed me, and now I'm safe." He cowered. "Except from the older kids."

"They, too, struggle to cope."

Jacob nodded. "I know."

"You are wise for such a small fry." Mac mussed the boy's hair. A cold wave of sadness washed over him at the realization of lost innocence, lost childhoods, lost and hopeless futures.

MAC FOUND A PLACE away from the campsite to instruct Jacob on defensive moves. "The first thing you'll need to do is go after the leader. Once you quash him, the others will be reluctant to challenge you." Jacob nodded. "What I'm going to teach you is about controlling your opponents, knocking them off-balance, using their momentum against them. Okay?"

Jacob stared up at Mac expressionless, waiting for the next set of instructions. Mac twisted his lips, not convinced Jacob comprehended what he was trying to convey.

"Come here." Mac placed Jacob a few feet in front of him. "I am going to go for you." Mac grabbed a good piece of Jacob's collar and gently tossed him to the ground.

Jacob glanced at Mac wide-eyed. Mac picked him off the ground. Now you try it on me."

Mac knelt to approximately Jacob's height. "Grab hold of my collar. Put your weight on your right foot and step back with the left. Stick your right elbow into my chest. That's right. Now tuck your left elbow into your ribs." Mac tried to push Jacob. "See how balanced you are?"

Jacob nodded.

"Shift your weight onto your left foot and sweep your right leg behind my knee. Push forward against my chest with your shoulder to break my balance. Now hook your right foot around and pull my leg out from under me."

Mac went with the fall. "Excellent. Let's try it again." Jacob clapped his hands in celebration. They continued to practice until he heard someone summon the kid.

"Jacob, I've been looking for you," Scarlet said. "It's time for bed."

"Sorry," Mac said. "I was showing the boy defensive skills."

Scarlet raised one eyebrow. "Maybe you could show me some of those moves later."

Mac felt his face flush. "Okay, kid, let's get you back." Mac escorted Jacob back to the wagon without waiting for Scarlet.

NINE
Anya

DEAD JAPANESE SOLDIERS LAY SPRAWLED ON THE ground. The back seat of the sedan held no prisoner. The resistance's attempt to rescue Zang had failed. One partisan fighter yelled obscenities while others wailed. Anya sympathized with the group's heartbreak and gave Longfu a mournful look.

Longfu's shoulders slumped and he sighed. "We'd best move on to avoid capture."

An unexpected voice blurted from within her car. "Anya. Anya. Come in. Over."

She raced to the car, grabbed the Handie-Talkie radio, and pushed the talk button. "Joe, what is it? Over."

"Did you get Zang? Over."

"It was a ruse. Over."

"There's a troop truck leaving the compound.

They're headed south out of town. Do you want me to pursue? Over."

Longfu straightened up like a soldier at attention and nodded.

Anya said, "Yes, we'll catch up with you. Over and out."

The resistance members piled into the back of the cargo truck while Anya and Longfu hopped into the cab. Longfu jammed the truck into gear, slammed down on the gas pedal, and sped to rendezvous with Joe.

"It's a good thing you had Joe stay behind to monitor the building, otherwise, we'd have never known about the ploy," Longfu said.

"I remember coming across a report at the War Department where Japanese had used a decoy in transferring American prisoners."

"This better be it." Longfu glanced at Anya. "We may never get another chance."

They had traveled less than twenty minutes when Anya pointed up ahead. "I think that's Joe by the side of the road."

Longfu maneuvered the car to a stop, rolled down the window, and stuck his head out. "Did you lose them?"

"No," Joe said. "They went onto this dirt road. I wasn't sure what to do, so I waited for you. There are two Japanese soldiers in the front seat, but the back of the truck is secured with a canvas flap."

Wushi approached Longfu with a furrowed brow. "If they're going where I think they are…" He swallowed hard. "We'd better hurry."

Longfu commandeered Joe's two-door sedan. "The rest of you wait here in case something goes wrong. We can't afford to have them return and report back to base."

Wushi pushed Anya aside, flipped the front seat forward, and jumped in the back before she was able to take the front seat. Longfu drove the car at a fast pace while he tried to avoid large potholes. At one point, the undercarriage took a knock so hard it punched a hole in the floorboard. Nevertheless, he continued. A swirl of dust and rocks kicked up behind them.

He nosed the car around a corner. They spotted the truck in the distance. Two men untied the back flap and flipped it over the top. Three soldiers bearing rifles leaped out.

Longfu scratched his head. "It looks like they are getting ready to go on patrol."

The butt of a rifle pushed out a blindfolded man with his hands tied behind his back. He tumbled to the ground and landed face first in the dirt. A fourth soldier hopped out of the truck and kicked at him to get up.

"It's Zang." Wushi leaned forward between the

seats. Anya felt his hot breath on her neck.

"They plan to execute him," Wushi said.

Longfu backed the car off the road. "Wushi and I will head up the road. Anya, contact the others and tell them to get the hell down here fast."

Anya relayed the message then slit the other side of her dress open to allow better mobility. She inhaled hard when she caught up to Longfu, more from anxiety than overexertion. The three ducked on their knees in the brush and watched the Japanese drag Zang to an open area.

"What should we do?" Anya said.

"Surprise is our only ally. We are out-manned and out-gunned." Longfu paused for a second. "Wushi, you circle around to the left. I'll go right. Anya, remain here until you see me signal."

The Japanese were in position. Five knelt on one knee with rifles butts pressed against their shoulders all pointed at Zang. The one soldier on his feet started a countdown.

Anya wiped the shimmer of sweat from her palms and waited as the others got into position. Longfu raised his hand as the sound of the attack force roared like thunder.

The truck's engine noise distracted the firing squad. Each man turned, then stood. They opened fire on the resistance. Wushi, Longfu, and Anya returned fire from their hidden positions. The soldiers scattered. Longfu shot one enemy in the chest. Anya got off a few rounds, but the gun pulled to the right and she missed her target.

Joe and the others sped to the action. They stopped a meter behind the Japanese truck and rushed out. Gunshots flew in all directions. Several shots pinged off the truck, others dug into nearby trees.

Within seconds, the deafening noise ceased. The gunfire stopped. Longfu motioned for everyone to move forward. They inched their way towards the dead soldiers except for Wushi who ran over to Zang.

"He's alive," Wushi yelled and helped Zang to his feet.

A shot rang out. Zang jerked and dropped to the ground. Anya swung around in the direction of the shot. A Japanese soldier up on his elbow, gun in hand, was positioned to fire again. She returned direct shots to his chest. She turned back to Zang and glanced over to Wushi. She saw him smile at her.

BACK AT THE COMPOUND a woman tended to Zang's wound. Several partisan fighters hovered as she wrapped a makeshift sling, from someone's white tunic, around his bandaged shoulder.

Anya noticed him wince when he sat upright. Zang's appearance set her aback. He did not display typical Chinese characteristics. The first thing that struck her was his blue eyes. His nose was sharper and he had a lighter tone to his skin. Even his tall physique, when he stood, surprised her. Zang caught her eye and heads rotated her way. A slight tremble ran through her body, and she fidgeted with her top shirt button as he approached.

He bowed and spoke to her in Mandarin. "I am Zang Koonings." There was a long pause. "You are probably wondering how a Chinese came to have such a last name."

Anya nodded.

"My father was a Dutch diplomat and my mother—his concubine."

Anya cast a shy smile. "China has been inhabited by many nations. It's due to her endurance that her culture has survived." She extended her hand. "Anya Pavlovitch. I am pleased to make your acquaintance."

"The pleasure is mine." He bowed.

Anya's cheeks flushed.

"Pavlovitch. That's Russian? Russian aristocracy isn't it?"

She declined to accept the significance. "I am now a citizen of the United States."

"I want to thank you for your part in my rescue."

"To thwart the Japanese is a delight," she said

with a slight bow.

"We can always use another soldier in our cause. They tell me you were recently in Shanghai. What brings you to Shinjing?"

"We narrowly escaped Japanese internment. I am now waiting for orders from Honolulu. In the meantime, I'm trying to find news about a comrade. I believe he may be dead, but there is a slight possibility he may be a prisoner of the Japanese. Either way, I need to find out."

"Maybe we can help. We have many contacts throughout China."

Anya admired Zang's soft-spoken authoritative approach contrary to Mac's cantankerous manner. She understood why so many were not only willing to follow him but risk their lives to save him.

"I've been told that you are handy with a weapon," he said.

"She killed a man," Joe chimed in. "Other than today."

"Only winged him. He died from another's bullet."

"Do you have experience with a rifle?" Zang said.

"Some."

"How about a rifle with a grenade attached?"

TEN
Mac

MAC HAD FOUND SOLACE FROM THE CONSTANT racket of the children's clamor. The gang had all gone to pick berries, and he used the opportunity to contemplate how to track down Dai Li. Mathew said they were a day or two from the main road that would lead to Chungking. He believed he had enough yuan to hire a guide when he arrived.

Mac stretched out inside the covered wagon and let his mind wander. He scanned the slits in the canvas and scratched his arm where a welt had developed. His eyes moved along, then stopped. He jerked up on his elbows and swallowed hard. In the far corner was Scarlet's sunhat. She never ventured into daylight without it. *Had she forgotten it…on purpose?*

The wagon flap flew open exposing the

afternoon sun. There stood Scarlet. Her golden hair cascaded in curls down her front. Her red lips looked like she had painted them with rouge. Her alabaster skin held a warm glow. Mac knew in an instant trouble was a-brew.

"Hello there," she said and climbed into the wagon. "Mind if I join you?"

Mac tried to scramble to his feet and exit. "I was just getting ready to…"

She pushed him and he fell back. She laughed then maneuvered herself on top of him.

"Scarlet." He pushed her away. "Mathew and the children may return any moment."

She bounced back. "They're far from here and won't return for hours."

Mac pulled one of her arms from around his neck. A second later, another arm was on him. "What are you, an octopus?"

She giggled.

"You have to stop." Mac's insistence seemed to encourage her as she continued to paw at him.

"You're acting like a naughty school girl."

"Oh I am, very naughty." She played with her curls. "I see willingness in those sultry blue eyes."

The silliness of it appeared absurd to Mac. She is not yet out of her teens, he thought. He wanted to laugh at her foolishness but feared it would egg her on. Scarlet had not been the only woman to make advances on him. There was a period in his life when he would have taken advantage of the situation, but he owed Mathew for taking him in.

He decided to take a different tactic. "Let's say we go ahead with this tryst. Do you plan to leave your husband and follow me?"

"It would be so much fun." She clapped.

"I'm going to kill a man. Do you find that fun?"

Her brow furrowed and she recoiled.

"Your duty is to stand by your husband. I can't have any part of whatever fantasies you've cooked up in that dizzy head of yours."

Scarlet's face raged red, and she raised her hand to slap him. Mac caught her arm in midair. At that minute, children's laughter echoed in the distance. The distraction allowed Mac to slide out the back of the wagon.

Mathew and the children had reached the campsite as Scarlet climbed out. Mac noticed that she fidgeted with her top blouse button. He watched Mathew's eyes shift between his wife and himself. Mac decided to follow the children with their berry-stained faces. He half-turned to see Mathew take hold of Scarlet's arm. She threw off his grasp and stomped away.

MAC SQUATTED NEXT TO the girls and watched the boys set up for kickball. He spotted Jacob mingling with the other boys. Jacob was not the shortest of the bunch, but certainly the boniest. His gaunt cheekbones and oversized clothes made him look even thinner.

Jacob reminded Mac of Joe who had also been raised by missionaries. All Jacob needed was a pair of wire-rimmed spectacles and they would be brothers. A sudden chill ran through Mac's body. *Jacob is nothing like Joe.*

The game began. The pitcher rolled an inflated rubber ball to a tall boy who stood behind a dirt-outlined home plate. He kicked the ball into outfield and was able to advance to second base. A lack of suitable outfielders made the advancement easier.

Pigtailed girls giggled and pointed at the boy, then cupped their hands over each other's ears and exchanged secrets. Mac reflected about his young daughter and longed to see her. He promised himself it would be soon.

Shouts from the pitch team razzed Jacob as he approached home plate. Mac hoped he would ignore them. The first pitch rolled past him before he could kick it. He was able to connect with the second pitch. Unfortunately, it landed in foul territory. The boys relentlessly harassed him.

One more pitch remained. If he failed it would be a strike out. Mac pulled his legs to his chest and rested his chin on his knees. The ball neared Jacob.

He pulled his leg back and made a solid connection. It flew at the pitcher. The pitcher, not expecting the ball, failed to catch it in mid-air. It dropped to his feet. He immediately grabbed the ball and hurled it to first base. The ball smacked Jacob in the head and bounced off him. He fell on his face. Mac had an urge to help him, but knew that would be a mistake.

Jacob seemed dazed as he stood. The baseman howled with laughter and screamed he was out. Jacob ran at the pitcher, formed a fist, and swung. He had forgotten everything Mac had taught him. The two boys wrestled to the ground. The rest of the players huddled around and cheered them on.

The ruckus caused Mathew and Scarlet to rush over and stop the fight. Mathew separated the boys and insisted they shake hands. They refused. Mathew untangled their folded arms and put their hands together.

Jacob hung his head and walked next to Mac. Mac put an arm around the boy. "You forgot the most important rule. Never, never, never lose your temper in a fight. It gives your opponent the advantage."

Jacob nodded.

"We'll work on it," Mac said. Out of the corner of his eye, Mathew gave him a disheartened expression. He asked Jacob to join the other children as Mathew approached.

"Let's walk," Mathew said.

They strolled a distance before Mathew spoke. He rubbed his chin and cleared his throat. "Scarlet told me what happened earlier."

Mac tensed up, he could only imagine what that *femme fatale* had said. He sensed Mathew's uneasiness, the way he stammered and was unable to make direct eye contact. Mac believed it best not to respond just let him get the words out.

"I am not a stupid man, Mr. Benson. I know a little something about my wife's character. I'm going to say this was her doing and end it at that. She is young and, therefore, reckless and impetuous. When she comes of age, she will bear my children and find her place. But for now, she is saddled with a man whose first obedience is to serve God." He removed his hat and wiped the sweat from his brow and receding hairline. "Her devotion may not be strong, but in time she will come to see things differently."

Mac did not believe the preacher's last statement. He had known women like Scarlet, and their spots never changed. He did, however, admire Mathew's goodness. He was not sure he would be as forgiving if the tables were turned.

They continued to walk along the path where the weeds grew tall. Mac plucked a long blade of grass and chewed on the end. "A woman can rip a man's guts right out of him without a thought," Mac said. "That's why I love the military. It's regular, organized, and straight forward."

Mathew smiled. "To love yourself, to have the compassion for others, to accept suffering is a part of life. That is, when you are truly alive."

"It is hard to love your enemy when you are at war."

"It takes a strong person, but even the strongest of men have a moment of fatigue."

"Mathew, you are a sage."

"I understand that you taught Jacob how to fight," Mathew said.

Mac nodded.

"The boy needs to learn that words are more powerful than fists." His voice remained quiet yet somber. "My wife tells me your aim is to kill a man."

Mac wanted to kick himself for divulging that to Scarlet. "It's why I am here in China."

"I believe you are an honorable man, but I think it is time for us to part ways. A crossroad is within hours from here. If you take the road to the right, it will lead you to Chungking. Our journey leads us on a different path."

"I apologize," Mac said. Only a handful of times had he used those words. This time he meant it. "Can I say goodbye to the boy?"

"It might be best if you simply left." Mathew patted Mac on the shoulder. "There was a reason you came into our lives. It may not have been for your sake alone. I will pray for your soul that you find your answers."

ELEVEN
Anya

ANYA'S FEET SLOSHED THROUGH RAINWATER that leaked onto the basement floor of the resistance's base camp. Water stains zigzagged down every dank misshapen wall, and mold grew on anything that did not move. Wrapped in a blanket, she wiped her wet nose on its satin edge. "When will the rain let up?"

"There's a slight chance the clouds may part today." Zang repositioned his injured arm in the sling. "We need to go over the plan for tomorrow once more."

Anya exhaled an exasperated sigh. They had already rehearsed more than a dozen times.

"Besides me," Zang said, "you are the only ones here who know how to properly use a rifle. And with this bum wing, I couldn't hit the side of a pagoda."

"I know what to do." Her stomach growled and she rubbed it. "But I need to eat before I blow up something."

Zang hollered to the group, "Someone get Miss Pavlovitch a cup of tea."

A resistance fighter approached Zang and whispered into his ear, then handed him a folded piece of paper. Zang unfolded it and read it. He gave Anya a quizzical look.

Anya accepted the tea handed to her and took a long sip.

"We've heard from a source in the Hubei province," Zang said. "They report that a tall, dark-haired European might be American. They didn't know for sure. He was reported to have escaped from an angry mob of villagers along with missionaries several days ago."

Anya's heart pounded. *Could he be alive?* She remembered Mac's gun in the hands of a Japanese soldier. She had been sure they had executed him. "Provoking a village enough to run him out of town—that sounds like Mac. I'll bet they chased him with clubs and pitchforks."

She had not calculated Mac into the equation. She questioned her next move. "How far is that from here?"

"About four hundred kilometers to the west," Zang said. "It's close to Chungking. I believe that's where you said your comrade is headed."

From the other side of the room, Anya saw Joe and Longfu whispering. At one point Joe gave her a sullen glance, then half-turned away. She put it at the back of her mind to talk with him later.

"I must get another message off." She had to inform Atwater that her earlier message was false and Mac might be alive and in route to complete his mission.

ANYA ONCE AGAIN SPORTED her Chinese apparel and bamboo hat to blend into the crowd. She was relieved to see that the rain had subsided. However, the dark overcast sky appeared threatening. Hordes of people, bicycles, and rickshaws scurried to get tasks completed before another downpour. She and Zang made their way across a busy street and picked up the pace. It was vital that they were on time to rendezvous with the weapons merchant.

Skewered meat on a stick, flatbreads, and flavored rice lingered in the air from street vendors. Anya passed a woman using two meal spatulas to stir a white mixture in a large black wok.

A barefooted, lanky man pulled his rickshaw while his oversized passenger indulged on sweets. The scowl on his face expressed his dismay. Besides people, cycle rickshaws hauled coal, lumber, and dry goods. A bicyclist clipped Zang's slung arm. He held up his good fist and shouted at the man. "These people have no concept of others' space. I'd go after him and clock him, if we had the time."

Anya stepped back. "You sound like an American."

"They play low budget English movies in almost every theatre." He chuckled. "You pick things up."

"Can we stop and get something to eat at one of these street vendors?"

Zang shook his head. "The oil they use to fry their food once resided in a truck or motorcar. The food is retrieved from garbage bins behind restaurants and the meat well…it's not anything you would want to eat."

Anya no longer felt the pangs of hunger.

Zang stopped steps before the entrance to a rickshaw shop and placed his arm out to stop her.

"What?" Anya said.

Zang scanned the display window. "It's okay. The golden Buddha is present."

"What?"

"The Buddha is our signal that the coast is clear."

Zang led the way and Anya followed close behind. Inside, rickshaws flooded the floor. A surplus hung from the wall and dangled off the ceiling. There were green, pink, yellow, but mostly black pull and cycle rickshaws. One impressive red rickshaw had tassels that hung off the edges of an elaborate embroidered canopy.

Zang's brow furrowed. "Wushi, I am surprised to see you. I thought you were helping the others setup counter-measures."

"Too many men for the job," he scowled. "My services are better used to assist you here."

Anya noticed Wushi give her a stern eye. His over concern for Zang made her reflect upon the similarity of Joe's and Shelley's relationship.

The shop owner, who appeared well over a hundred with his pruned face and gnarled hands, shuffled to the front door, locked it, and flipped over the sign to read closed. He waved them to follow. In a storage room, the old man removed a rug that exposed a trap door. He struggled to pull on the heavy iron handle. Zang and Wushi assisted him. The three of them descended several wooden steps. Anya waited topside.

"Anya," Zang hollered. "Get down here. You need to try out the weight."

She descended and coughed from wisps of dust that floated in the air. The cramped space reminded her of a root cellar. Instead of canned fruits and vegetables, it was a war chest of guns, grenades, swords, knives, and unfamiliar metal gadgets.

"Try this one." Zang handed her a rifle.

"A Mauser." She rubbed her hand along the

metal barrel. "These are as common as hookers on the street." She flung the strap over her shoulder and stared down its barrel, pointed it at Wushi.

"Are you barmy," he said.

She ignored his complaint. "It'll work."

Zang motioned to the merchant to include it in the total.

Anya dismantled the rifle and they each placed pieces in their deep coat pockets along with the other items that Zang selected.

THEY SNAKED THROUGH THE STREETS, alleyways, over rail tracks, and under a bridge trestle. It crossed her mind after an hour that they might be lost. Zang stopped in an industrial area surrounded by warehouses. "We're here," he said.

They climbed the five flights of stairs to the rooftop across from the target. The sky had turned dark enough to call it night and sporadic raindrops trickled. They each gave pieces of the rifle to Anya who reassembled it.

"Where did you learn so much about guns?" Zang said.

"My father was a military man. While my mother taught me how to cook, my father drilled me on weapons."

Wushi snatched the rifle from Anya. He attached a metal cylinder to a spigot on the rifle's muzzle then handed it back to her.

"I need you to aim at the second level. That's where the ammo is housed," Zang said.

Anya knelt on one knee and rested the weapon on the building ledge for balance. She peered down the barrel to find her mark and nestled the butt of the rifle into her shoulder. "Okay, I'm ready."

Anya flinched when a cast iron pineapple crossed her line of sight. Wushi unhooked the grenade pin and placed it in the tube attached to the rifle. The added weight caused her to lose her mark, but she regained it quickly enough. Her index finger hard on the trigger, she counted to three and fired.

An initial explosion blew out the windows. Shattered glass flew onto the street. The blast wave hit her straight on and knocked her over. A succession of several loud blasts erupted. Flames shot out from all sides of the second floor.

On the street, soldiers scurried out of the building from all corners like gangsters during a raid. A machine gun nest erupted from the roof across the way. Everyone ducked for cover.

The gunfire ceased. Anya peered over the edge. The damaged building swayed several feet in either direction. The second level buckled. Within seconds, the entire four-story structure collapsed. A plume of dust mixed with debris rose to meet her.

"We can't escape the way we came," Zang said.

"We'll have to jump to another building,"

Anya's eyes widened as her fear of heights revealed itself. Zang jumped across the five-foot gap between the buildings and landed with little difficulty. He coaxed Anya to follow. Self-preservation forced her to act. *Just don't look down.* She dropped her weapon and leaped across. She had made it with less than a meter to spare. Wushi also made it.

They ran to the next ledge. The distance appeared twice that from the previous building. Anya's knees wobbled. Zang took a running start and landed within inches. Anya motioned for Wushi to go next. He caught his foot on the lip of the ledge of the other building and fell face forward. Zang caught him before he crashed to the dirt-laden ground.

Anya inhaled a serious breath, gulped, and leaped. As her foot left the rooftop, she slipped on loose gravel. She knew the moment of lift-off she was in trouble. She managed to clear her mind and stretch out her arms. Her fingers grabbed the edge of the building. The weight of her dangling body caused her grip to give way. Adrenaline coursed through her veins. Wushi grabbed her arm as the last of her fingers held on. Their eyes fixed on each other. She thought about how much this man hated her and now her life was in his hands. His grip slipped. She remained calm and trusted that he would do the right thing. She felt herself rise up. Zang had grabbed the other arm, and together they pulled her to safety.

They wiped the sweat from their brows with relief. The crash of a door that slammed open drew their attention. A Japanese soldier burst onto the roof. He aimed at Zang. Wushi threw himself in front of Zang as the gun discharged. Wushi collapsed. Zang returned two shots and dropped the soldier.

Zang knelt beside his friend, placed his face in his lap, and caressed it. The clouds released moisture and rain pelted them. Anya pulled her coat over her head. Zang gently rested Wushi's head on the ground and jumped to his feet.

"We have to go," he said.

"Do we just leave him here?"

"There is nothing more we can do for him."

Anya and Zang fled down the fire escape and headed for shelter.

TWELVE
Anya

ANYA AND ZANG RETURNED, RAIN DRENCHED, TO base camp sometime after twenty-two hundred hours. The news of Wushi's death hit the group hard. The place held a quiet eeriness. The only sound came from the slurry that ran down the walls. The troops all huddled near Zang, who stood in the middle of the room.

"Wushi was a good fighter," he said. Cheers erupted in unison. "Always the first to volunteer for an assignment. Always the first to draft a plan to disrupt the enemy. Always the first to aid a fellow comrade." His voice broke.

Someone yelled, "Hurrah."

"He will never be forgotten," Zang said. They all raised one fist overhead and bowed their heads in silence.

Anya lifted her arm in solidarity. She recalled how Wushi had sacrificed himself to save Zang and questioned if she could ever do the same. She harbored remorse for jokingly pointing the rifle at him earlier.

"We must take extra precautions. They will be scouring the city for revenge," Zang said. "We need to attack again while the enemy is confused and distracted. A manufacturing plant on the outskirts of town requires our attention. We'll map out our next plan tomorrow. Until then, let's all get some sleep."

As the group disbursed, Anya approached Zang. "For all our differences, I believe Wushi and I came to understand each other. I regret I never thanked him for saving my life." She paused. "He seemed very attached to you."

"I saved his life." Zang displayed a half smile. "About a year ago….it was happenstance that a few scouts and I stumbled upon him. We'd been tracking game in the woods and on our way home. I think we all smelled it meters before we saw it. I'll never forget the stench. Along what we believed to be a deserted dirt road, we encountered a mound of dead bodies in a ditch. It was as if someone had tossed out garbage. I stood unable to move. Several got sick. Some cried. Others lost temporary use of their legs and fell to the ground.

"In the mangled horror, I saw movement and

shouted to the others. Without thought, we jumped in and began to pull away corpses. At the bottom was Wushi. A bullet had gone through his ribcage and another lodged in his leg. He told us later Japanese soldiers had rounded up several men and boys they believed were Communist sympathizers. They lined them up beside the ditch and murdered them. He was one of the first hit and fell in. Several other bodies toppled in and hid him. They continued to shoot at them in the ditch. Wushi said he lay still even when a bullet hit his leg."

Zang sighed. "He was a good fighter and my friend."

Anya touched his forearm and gave it a light squeeze. "I don't think I shall ever forget him."

"None of us will." A man from across the room flagged over Zang.

Anya saw Joe out of the corner of her eye. She remembered him speaking to Longfu earlier. The intense look on his face made her curious to find out what they had discussed. She attempted to engage Joe but Zang impeded her path.

"A telegraph message is coming in from Honolulu," he said.

The translator was still receiving the message as they entered the room. Anya smiled. *This looks like the same drab quarters back at San Francisco.* It had been well over a month since she had been in her office in San

Francisco. To her, it seemed years. Paval's face flashed before her. She had lived with him for eight years, until he took his life just before she was to leave on assignment. *Why had he done it?* Anya held back her tears.

"Everything all right?" Zang said.

"Echoed memories."

"I wanted to thank you again for your part in today's operation," he said. "I know things didn't go exactly as planned."

"Yeah, like the whole building collapsing and one of our soldiers dying," she said.

He grunted in agreement and focused on her eyes. "We could use your talents."

She fingered the snakehead pendant against her clavicle and thought about the message that required Atwater's attention at the War Department. "I wish I could stay but it's not possible."

The translator finished his decipher and handed her the paper.

```
Vital, locate agent.
Elimination sanctioned.
All other orders rescinded.
Dispose G² message.
                          ERA.
```

Anya caught her breath and her hand moved to her chest as she read the second line, elimination sanctioned. It would require stopping Mac from completing his mission, even if it meant killing him.

She sighed at the prospect of what it would take to locate Mac in Chungking, but she did not want to shirk her responsibility. She wondered when it came down to it…could she…pull the trigger against a friend, an ally, and leave a child without a father.

She had relayed to Atwater in her last communication the crucial message Guy Gilot had given her, and now he was telling her to destroy it. *If the information is no longer of value and Mac's orders are to abort his mission, then the U.S. government and Dai Li's relationship has improved.* She would burn the concealed microdot but keep the snake pedant. It had been the last thing Guy had given her.

Zang held onto Anya's forearm. "I meant what I said. Now that Wushi is gone, I need a good right hand." He looked at his injured arm. "Make that a left hand." His intense gaze made her fidget.

She pulled free and pointed to the paper. "You see these initials? Edmund Robert Atwater—my boss. This is my duty."

"We could use you. I've lost one man and recently had another turn traitor.

"Traitor?" Anya said.

"He was a little guy about your height. He slipped throughout the city and scavenged for us. If we needed a car, camera, or a special weapon that others didn't have, it would somehow magically appear. We found out later that he owed a lot of money to a ruthless bookie. To pay off his debt he became a mole for the Japanese. He managed to escape but not before we were able to leave an identifying mark on his face." Zang placed his index finger on his cheekbone then dragged it down to his chin. "He'll surface again, and when he does, he'll get what's coming to him." Zang pleaded with Anya. "We need you here."

"You can keep Joe." She went to leave and stopped. "There is nothing you can say that will change my mind."

"At least sleep on it," He called out to her.

Anya was not ready for sleep. Instead, she scoured the place in search of Joe. He was leaning against a wall talking to Longfu. They both walked away. She called out to Joe but he ignored her. She shouted his name again which caused her voice to echo down the hall. Joe turned and waited but Longfu kept on.

"I've wanted to talk with you all day," she said.

"What about?"

"I saw you and Longfu earlier, and just now, in what seemed like a serious conversation. You gave me a look that caused me to think there might be an issue. Is there anything you want to tell me?"

"No." He shrugged. "Nothing."

Anya sensed something strange in his manner. "You know how much I hate secrets."

Joe diverted his eyes and wrung his hands. "There's nothing. Honest."

"Okay, I trust you'd let me know."

He nodded and shifted his stance.

"I've been ordered to head out for Chungking. You are free to stay."

Joe stood upright. "I have to come."

"Have to?"

"You need me. I know the way. I know the people. I know what dangers lay ahead."

His staccato pleas made her wary. She had not forgotten that he had surrendered her to the Green Gang, although her gut told her to trust him. "We leave in the morning."

ANYA AND JOE READIED THEMSELVES for Chungking early the next day. She wanted to avoid another encounter with Zang. The partisan fighters and their vigilant cause would remain in her heart. However, she would not miss the musty leaky basement.

She turned the corner to ascend the stairs and ran into Zang.

"Stealing away before dawn without a word?" he said.

"I think we've said all there is to say. I wish I could stay but…"

"You can't or won't," Zang said.

She wrinkled her nose at him. Joe appeared over Anya's right shoulder.

Zang's blue eyes widened. "I thought Joe planned to stay."

"Miss Anya needs me."

"Come. I want to show you something," Zang said.

Anya and Joe followed him up the stairs and outside. A beam of early light blinded her before she could shade her eyes. She focused on a two-seat buckboard wagon with a dapple-gray horse hitched to it.

"We wanted to give you a car but figured where you're going there'd be no petrol stations."

"I don't know what to say." She put her hands to her face.

"It's a small gesture of thanks," Zang said. Resistance members circled around.

"It's loaded with supplies." He handed her a rifle and shells. "Figure this might come in handy."

Along with her Beretta, she now felt fully armed. "Thanks." Tears welled up in her eyes. "Thank you all."

"Well," he kicked the ground with the toe of his shoe. "If you should ever end up in Shinjing, you know where to find me—us."

Anya leaned in and kissed Zang on both cheeks. "You never know," she winked.

Several members teased Zang with hoots and howls.

"Come on Joe, we're off to rescue a man from his fate."

THIRTEEN
Mac

WHITE BILLOWY CLOUDS CARPETED THE SKY AS Mac trudged along a desolate dirt road. The days had been without incident since he parted from the missionaries. Memories of Jacobs's gaunt little body as he grappled to learn to defend himself cast a smile on Mac's face. He believed he had deserted the boy. His smile evaporated. It crossed his mind that he had done the same to his daughter. He promised himself to do better by his family when he returned home.

An ache in his feet from the rocky road caused him to stop and rest. Mac plopped down on a boulder, removed his shoes, and massaged his feet. He wished he had absconded with one of Mathew's donkeys. A grumble from his stomach took precedence over his soreness. He opened the bag of food Mathew had packed for him. It would be ample until he reached Chungking, two more days according to Mathew. He bit into a baozi bun and tried to eat slowly, but it had been twenty-four hours since his last meal. He devoured the soft dough combined with the crunchy vegetables with the least amount of chewing involved.

Mac eyed the hilly terrain ahead with its steep acclivity. Years of agricultural carving had evolved the hillside into a terrace of varying shades of green from mint to kale. The last few rays of sunlight illuminated the lush fields. A trail zigzagged up alongside the rice paddies. Black-clad figures dotted the different levels as they worked the land. Mac had seen pictures of this topography in a National Geographic magazine, but to see this century-old splendor in person made him pause. *No war appears to have sliced its way into this valley.*

Mathew had said that once on the other side of the mountain, it was a day's walk to Chungking. A burst of energy took hold at the prospect of confronting Dai Li. His mind said plod on, but his feet refused to obey. Twilight fast approached, and it would be best to wait until first light to make the arduous climb. Tall weeds parted as he hiked through a field to an untended graveyard. He hid behind the stone monuments beneath the firs to avoid any patrol or nosey neighbors.

THE SOUND OF A cocked hammer woke Mac. He rolled over to feel the cold iron barrel of a gun against his cheek. *Damn.* The graveyard had not been as abandoned as he had believed. The morning light silhouetted three men dressed in black. One man peered down and spoke to him in Chinese.

Mac did not reply and the gunman stepped aside. A second man tapped his fingers on Mac's chest. "You English?"

"American," Mac said.

"Where you go?'

Mac pointed to the mountain. "Chungking."

The man rubbed his fingers together then held out his hand. "Yuan."

Mac shrugged.

"Dollars to climb mountain."

"I have no money." Mac tried to stand, but the butt of a rifle on his chest pushed him back.

The extortionists grouped together and exchanged words. Guns remained pointed at him. Mac contained a snicker at their clothes. To him, they looked like movie extras in a western with their black shirts, pants, and cowboy hats. *The only thing they're missing are six-shooters strapped to their legs.*

The group broke up and one gunman motioned for Mac to stand. He searched him and found the gun he had taken from the previous holdup. Mac had tucked his money sack in a place he believed no man would touch. He could always find a weapon.

"We take you."

"I can find my own way," Mac said.

"We go," the bandit said.

The intense gaze into their beady eyes told him he was not going to win this argument. The three ascended the misty hillside on horseback. Mac was on foot with bound hands. A long rope tethered to a saddle horn pulled him along.

Halfway up the mountain Mac stumbled and fell. The horse did not stop. It dragged him several feet while the kidnapers laughed. When it did finally stop and Mac got up, he spit out dirt that had collected in his mouth.

Most of the journey over the cold mountain had chilled him to the marrow. The warmth of the late afternoon sun on the other side was a welcomed relief. In the distance was a tall stone wall. Unsure what to expect upon his arrival, Mac figured it would not be in his favor.

They passed by wooden gate doors and entered the compound. Small buildings with pitched roofs encircled the town. A large water well lay at its center. A few leafless tree branches held early buds. Children frolicked as women dressed in simple garb eyed them.

They dismounted as an elderly man supported by a tall stick walked toward them. He wore a long, black robe with a small round black cap atop his head. His white queue almost touched the ground. A bandit spoke to the old man. Mac was certain they were plotting against him.

"No worry, we take care you," one man said then slapped Mac on the back.

"That's what I'm afraid of," Mac uttered under his breath.

Several people swarmed around him. Some spat at him. Others growled and grumbled. One woman poked him with a stick as if testing a roast. Children teased and lunged at him, but he remained motionless. He did not want to evoke an unnecessary confrontation.

Two of the bandits grabbed him and dragged him to a small stone building. They pushed him in, then slammed and locked the door behind him.

"You write people in Chungking. Get money, then go free," a voice said.

From outside the cobwebbed cell, Mac heard their insolence and mockery. "We drive you out of China you foreign devil…you and your Jesus."

My Jesus? "He's not my Jesus," Mac yelled at a wall opening the size of a small window several arm lengths above his head. "I'm no missionary." He then muttered, "You infidels."

He leaned against the wall and sighed. *Great. Miles away from Chungking and I get kidnapped. Anya won't be coming to rescue you this time, bucko.*

The harassment from outside continued. Stones pelted the side of the building. A couple flew through the opening and landed a few inches from him. Mac moved to the far corner to avoid a blow. He squatted with his back against the wall and thought about how to escape. He stared at the wall opening and decided to wait until the protesters had gone to bed, then try to reach it.

The clank of the door unlocked and opened with a creak. One of his captors put a bowl on the ground along with paper and charcoal. "Write for freedom," he grunted then left.

Mac walked over to inspect it. It was rice but when he picked it up, it moved. "Maggots." He threw the bowl across the room, which caused it to shatter and its contents to scatter. A series of squeals alerted him that he was not alone. "Rats. I hate rats."

Mac could stand up to Sun's torture, but when it came to rats, fear replaced courage. He recalled the vision of himself as a young boy. His older brothers would hold him down and try to feed him a live rat. It squirmed to free itself as they held it by its tail less than in inch over his mouth. Mac shuddered.

A GIBBOUS MOON'S LIGHT allowed Mac to make out the various stones used to construct the cell wall. He rubbed his hand along the surface. The stones were rough in spots with a slight bump enough to anchor his hand and foot, then lift himself up to a higher level. He felt around for a third bulge when his right foot gave way, and he crashed to the floor of the cell. The second try ended the same. There were only so many solid bumps, and he was running out of them. Mac made one last attempt. He carefully placed his right foot in position then pulled himself up and placed his left foot on a lump. He scaled the uneven wall until he felt the ledge of the opening. He gripped it with the fingers of both hands and hoisted himself up onto his elbows. No one wandered about outside, not even a sentry. *They must believe this is escape proof. I'll show them.*

Mac twisted his body and pushed his way through the opening but he could not budge. His shoulders were too broad. Even after pounding the edges, it would not give way. Exhausted, he dropped to the ground. He closed his weary eyes, ready to try again in a moment.

MAC OPENED HIS EYES. "Damn." He was angry with himself for having fallen asleep. He would have to withstand another day in the rat-infested cell to make his escape.

The rants from outside commenced again. The cell door opened and a man entered. He scanned the room and eyed the shattered bowl. A smile stretched across his face. Mac crossed his arms and grunted.

The guard picked up the paper and charcoal and threw it at Mac. "You write."

Mac sat still for a quiet second then picked them up. He scribbled a few words then handed it back to him. The guard looked at it, turned the paper upside down and continued to study it, then left.

Mac laughed aloud. He had written, *Help me, I am being held prisoner by this man.* His laughter ceased at the realization of his predicament. He stood up and investigated the wall. *This is an old building. It must have a weak spot somewhere.*

He dug at the mortar with his fingers in several spots. He inched his way along the room, searching, prodding, and digging.

Sunlight started to fade when he discovered a point where the stone crumbled. In his excitement to free the stone, he failed to hear the cell door unlock. He swung around at the sound of the creak as the door opened. He positioned himself in front of the chipped-out section.

The guard placed a bowl down and left. Mac picked it up. It appeared edible. He slid three fingers into the gruel and pulled out a mouthful. It wasn't until he neared the bottom when he noticed movement. He dropped the bowl, spit out what was in his mouth, and coughed up the rest. Laughter howled from the other side of the door. Mac wiped his mouth on his shirtsleeve. He would get back at them by escaping.

It occurred to him that a large piece of the broken bowl would make a handy tool. Decades of dust filled his nostrils and made him sneeze. He used his shirt to cover his face. A rat crossed over his foot. He jumped, lost his balance, and fell to his knees. A sticky substance adhered to his hands when he used them to get back on his feet. "Shit." He sniffed his hands. "Literally." He wiped most of it off on the wall and resumed his dig.

One stone loosened. He grabbed its edges and pulled it out. He used the freed stone to pound out another stone, then another, and another.

The hole was large enough to peer outside. People covered themselves and ran screaming into their homes. Mac focused on the sky. The moon, now full, had transformed into a red ball. Secluded in the black sky, it glowed like a towering symbol. He had heard tales of unsavory acts during a blood moon. Knowing the superstitious nature of the Chinese, he seized the opportunity to increase the hole and squeeze free.

Mac dashed behind a barn. He darted from one building to the next. He was prepared to scale the town gate but in all the commotion, someone had forgotten to secure the door. Mac caught his breath before he made a run for it.

Halfway to the gate, he crossed paths with a woman who clutched a baby bundled in her arms. They both stopped and stared at each other. Mac placed his index finger to his lips. The mother screamed. Her scream caught the attention of villagers. Mac darted past her and through the gate.

A throng of angry men with torches pursued him as Mac ran into a forest. He was far enough ahead he was able to scamper up a bushy evergreen. He climbed high enough to hide himself from the torchlight. Mac assumed, like most people in search of something, they would not look up. When their lights were no longer visible, he climbed down and ran until exhaustion took hold. Hungry and his head about to explode, Mac collapsed in a field.

FOURTEEN
Anya

ANYA STRUGGLED TO HOLD ONTO THE HORSE'S reins, but the sweat on her hands from the afternoon heat made it impossible to maintain a tight grip. She and Joe sat in silence as the wagon wheels thumped along the rocky road to Chungking. An image of her firing pointblank at Mac whirled around in her mind like a tornado. To find Mac would be a challenge. But to kill him. She bit her lower lip. Where would she find the strength, the courage, the guts?

"What should we do, Joe?"

"About what, Miss?"

"Sorry, thinking out loud." She glanced his way with a wisp of a smile. "It's a funny world, isn't it?"

"In what sense?"

"Hunting the hunter."

"Not so funny."

The sky had turned muddy gray. "Doesn't look too friendly," Anya said. "We'd better find shelter."

She steered the buckboard along a narrow, well-worn path. The nettles along the side of the road were so tall they could pluck one without bending over. Fresh tracks in the soft soil signified recent visitors. "What do you think? Soldiers?"

"I see small footprints, most likely a child," he said. "It appears to be one or more families traveling."

Less than a mile later, they heard strange melodic sounds echo from ahead. Anya pulled on the horse's reins, then she and Joe climbed down. She tied the reins to a tree branch. The two moved forward. They peered through tall scrub careful to remain hidden. There were three vardo wagons. She had seen similar ones in Russia. Oversized wheels extended halfway up the sides of the tall structures. Two had canvas stretched over their curved frames. The largest, constructed entirely of wood, had a colorful design painted from top to bottom. Five steps led to a door where a young girl carrying a large bowl descended. Next to the wagon was a woman. The ends of her headscarf dangled from the side of her face. She wore a long full stripped skirt, a billowy white blouse, and print vest. She stirred a black pot that hung over an open fire. Several feet from her, a group of men wearing white turbans sat around a campfire and smoked from hookahs. A band of children chased a large black dog with a white chest.

"Luoli," Joe said. "You call them Gypsies. They originally came from the silk route. I thought they'd been chased out or slaughtered hundreds of years ago. It's believed they can see the future."

"These are probably descendants," Anya said. No sooner had the words spilled from her mouth than the dog caught their scent. He took off after them like a cheetah. Anya and Joe raced for their wagon. The dog clipped one of Joe's heels as he jumped onto the buckboard seat. The hound continued to bark and nip at Joe who used his shoe to fend it off while the horse reared and kicked at it with its hind legs.

Three men and a few children had followed. A burly man grabbed the dog by the collar and whipped it. The dog yelped and cowered. Another man grabbed the reins and calmed the horse.

They held little resemblance to the Chinese with their long, straight noses. One girl had green almond-shaped eyes and a reddish tinge to her hair. Trapped by grim faced men and a hostile dog, Anya tried to swallow, but her mouth was devoid of saliva. Joe sat next to her wide-eyed. Their arms touched and she felt him tremble.

The group parted as a woman pushed her way through with the spoon she had used to stir her pot.

She wore gold-hooped earrings and strands of colorful beads draped around her neck. A small red dot lay between her eyebrows. Her weathered face looked as dry as a reptile's skin. She spoke to the eldest man in a language Anya did not understand. She turned to Joe who shrugged. The old woman turned to Anya, her broad smile exposed a few missing teeth, and said in perfect Mandarin, "Please join us."

"I guess they are inviting us to eat with them," Anya said.

Joe said, "Why does she stare at me as though I was a tasty meal?"

"Maybe she has a crush," Anya winked. "I think we should join them."

Joe mumbled, "Something doesn't feel right." Anya ignored his complaint and nodded to the gypsy woman. A man holding the horse's halter led them to their campsite.

THE GLOW OF THE CAMPFIRE along with a few well-placed torches lit up a space about fifteen feet in diameter. They all sat in a circle around the fire. The black dog curled up at Joe's side.

"He's taken quite a shine to you," Anya said.

"He must have liked the taste of my shoe. Let's hope he turns out to be an ally." Joe petted the dog's head. His tail wagged in response.

A long-lashed maiden with her eyes lowered delivered plates of food. She had a metal brace strapped to her left leg and foot. It caused her to walk with a slight limp. Her hands shook when she handed the dish to Anya.

"What is your name?" Anya said.

The girl looked up. Her eyes shifted across the way as if to seek permission to speak. "Nadira," she said.

"Thank you, Nadira." Anya inhaled the aroma of exotic spices. Mixed together were cubed meat with rice and vegetables. Anya took a bite and exclaimed, "I have no idea what it is, but it's the best meal I've had in months."

A potbellied man with a scruffy beard fiddled a lively tune on his violin after the meal. Everyone clapped hands to the music. Tongues clacked as several slapped wooden spoons together in rhythm.

Anya clapped along in unison. "I love how everyone is involved."

"Something doesn't feel right," Joe said. "You don't know the reputation of Luoli."

"You worry too much. Besides, we know how to protect ourselves." She referred to the guns hidden in their wagon.

The old woman continued to eye Joe. He shifted in his seat. He nudged Anya. "Can we go to sleep now?"

She wanted to stay, but her empathy for Joe's uneasiness won over. They excused themselves and found shelter under their buckboard, protected from possible rain.

That night, images of a faceless person chasing her with a knife kept Anya from a restful sleep. During the night, she woke herself up panting in a cold sweat. At the hint of dawn, she arose to the smell of a sweet aroma. Through the spokes of the wagon wheel, she watched Nadira ladled hot liquid into small bowls.

"Feeling any better this morning?" Joe said. "I heard your fitful night."

"I could sleep for a month if not for the dreams," she said. His brow wrinkled. "Don't worry. It will pass."

They rustled themselves out from under the buckboard and ambled over to the fire. Nadira gave them each a cup. Tealeaves floated in the hot water. She poured a small stream of cold water over the cup, which caused the leaves to sink to the bottom. She pointed to the cup and told Anya when she finished she would tell her fortune.

Anya took the last sip, handed the cup to Nadira and sat cross-legged next to her. The girl took the cup careful not to disturb the sediment. She took it by the handle, rim upwards, and moved it in a circle rapidly three times from left to right. Next, she inverted it over the saucer until all the liquid drained. She studied the leaves for several minutes before speaking. "You are on a long journey."

Anya whispered to Joe in English, "I guess the wagon was the giveaway."

"You seek someone. This person is in danger."

Anya perked up and began to focus on her words.

"You are not the only one searching for this person. Others also seek."

Anya's brow furrowed and her lips pursed. "Joe, did you tell her about our mission?"

"No. Honest."

"You will give away something of great importance," Nadira said.

Anya placed the palm of her hand over the pendant.

"Wait." Nadira held up her hand. "Someone wants to harm you." Her hawkish stare sent a chill through Anya.

"Who?" Anya said.

"The leaves are not specific. They only tell of the events that will occur."

The blood left Joe's face and he trembled.

"What is it, Joe?"

"I should have mentioned this to you back in Shinjing, but I was afraid. Afraid how you might react."

"What?"

"Longfu said a man using the name of Sun Temujin was in search of a Russian woman."

"That's impossible." Her voice shook. "Mac shot him. We left him for dead in Shanghai."

"I am telling you what I was told and his description sounded accurate."

The hairs on Anya's arm stiffened and she jumped to her feet. Her legs went wobbly and she grabbed Joe's arm to steady herself.

"Is there anything else you've forgotten?"

Joe held up his right hand. "Swear that's all I know." He cowered. "Uh, one more thing."

"Yes."

"Sun is headed to Chungking."

Anya threw her arms in the air. "Of course he is." She placed her hands on her hips, paced, then stopped. "I guess we'd best be on our way and join everyone in Chungking."

Nadira lowered her head and pointed to Joe. "He must stay."

FIFTEEN
Mac

A SHARP PAIN BEGAN IN MAC'S HEAD THEN traveled throughout his body. The weight of a blanket warmed and soothed him. He stirred, opened one eye and then the other. A blurry diminutive figure of a man dressed in a black robe hovered overhead. "How are you feeling?" The figure spoke in English with a slight accent.

Light filtered through years of dirt from a four-paned window. Sweet aromatic scents filled his nostrils. Things came into focus. Transparent glass jars filled with strange dried leaves and twigs were stacked from ceiling to floor along two circular walls. He recalled seeing similar jars at a teashop in Shanghai. The other walls housed rows of books. Several stacks sat catawampus on the floor. "Where am I?" His words barely escaped.

"You are safe." The man held a pleasant smile.

Mac recalled his escape from the bandits before he had lost his breath and collapsed. He removed one arm from under the blanket and scratched the stubble on his chin. "How long?"

"Have you been here?"

Mac nodded.

"Two days. Before that, I do not know. I found you in a field a few miles from my house. Friends helped me carry you here. I believe you may have contracted an infection."

Mac's brow furrowed and his eyes narrowed. "I remember being surrounded by rats, coughing, and digging my way free."

"You most likely inhaled spores from rat droppings. The symptoms are similar to influenza yet more severe. I have plied you with an herbal remedy that has lowered your fever and should reduce the muscle ache."

Mac touched his forehead and felt no sign of a fever. "Where is here?"

"My home. It is near the great mountain city, Chungking."

Mac tried to prop himself up on his elbows, but his arms gave way.

"You are still too weak. It will take another day or two until you regain your strength."

Mac dozed off. Exhaustion had won over his

endless drive to find Dai Li—the assignment, the nemesis, and the triumph to his quest.

MAC WOKE WITH A JOLT and sat up in bed. It took him a moment to regain his senses. He noticed a long thick stick propped up in the corner and questioned its purpose. His host sat at a table, jars lined up from one end to the other. He removed a pinch from each jar, put it into a mortar and ground them up with a pestle. He then placed the powder into a small bowl, added hot water and sipped it.

"I'd like to know the name of my doctor so I may thank him," Mac said.

"Shen Ziya." He bowed.

"Nice to meet you. The name is Mac Benson." He yawned, laced his fingers behind his head, and leaned back.

"Your dreams are filled with angst, Mister Benson."

Mac sat up. "What did I say?"

"Nothing of consequence."

He sat back again. "I've been shot at, knocked unconscious, tortured, and locked up with rats. I think my dreams deserve a little anxiety."

"I suspect your life is like vinegar, sour and bitter. You need to seek the sweetness of harmony."

Mac guffawed. "No time for that."

"You have somewhere to go?"

"Yes, somewhere very important."

"Oh. Very important. I see." Shen seemed indifferent.

Restless in his confinement, Mac swung his legs over the edge of the bed and tried to stand, but fell. Shen lifted Mac's arm around his shoulder and helped him up. Together they shuffled across the wood-planked floor where Shen sat him in a chair next to a well-used worktable.

Shen ladled hot tea into a small porcelain bowl. "Drink." He handed Mac the bowl. "It will give you strength."

Mac took a sip then puckered his lips. The bitter taste reminded him of dandelion soup his mother made for him and his brothers when they were ailing from stomach or intestinal problems.

"Shen, tell me, why'd you bring a stranger into your home?"

"All manner of life is sacred and should be given equal respect. Man was put upon this earth to tend to those in need. The bird, the rabbit, the cow… even an American."

A crooked grin crossed Mac's face. "We eat many of those creatures. How does that make them our equal?"

"Beasts and birds are sentient beings. The bird in the sky or the cow in the field may have once been a mother, a sister, or perhaps a friend. Would you eat a brother?"

Mac rubbed his chin. "Well, there's one brother I'd consider." He studied the spiritual man in black. "I don't think I could give up having a juicy steak once in a while."

"I do not ask you to. I only ask that you think about it the next time you feed upon flesh."

Mac grunted then rose from his seat. He used the edge of the table for balance as he stretched his legs.

Shen sat in a high-back chair, his delicate hands rested in his lap. "We have been together these last few days and I have watched you struggle with yourself. There is a demon that tugs at your soul. If not expelled, it could destroy you."

"There are things you don't know about me," Mac said.

"You believe you seek something or someone but in fact you are in search of yourself."

"Maybe you're right." He raked his fingers through his tousled hair. "I have given my word and I'm not one to go back on it."

"It is honorable to keep your word, as long as it does not consume the goodness."

"Such as abandoning my wife and child?"

Shen remained quiet. Expressionless.

"I think about them often. I wonder how they are getting along without me. I wonder if they will take me back when I return. I wonder if I can live without them in my life."

A knock at the door caused Shen to rise and greet the visitor. Mac could not see whom, but heard raised voices. The tenor of Shen's voice sounded curt, yet respectful as he shut the door. He returned to his chair.

"What was that?" Mac glanced at the door.

"My neighbors are worried that your presence will cause them trouble."

"Tell them I am with the American Embassy and we work alongside the Chinese authorities."

"It is not that authority that concerns them. It is a local gang who blackmails them for protection."

"You don't pay?"

"I have no money, therefore no need of protection. They can do nothing to me."

"They can inflict pain."

"What is life without suffering?"

"Someone else said that to me recently." Mac remembered his conversation with Mathew before he asked him to leave.

"I would very much like to meet this person," Shen said.

"You two have a lot in common." Mac paused. "I plan to leave tomorrow. I am grateful for all you have done." Mac hobbled over to the bed and reached for his pouch. He pulled out a few yuan and gave them to Shen.

Shen put his hands inside his oversized sleeves. "I did not do this for payment but to honor my principles as a fellow human being."

Mac admired this little man with a heartfelt soul and wished he could be more like him and Mathew.

THE NEXT MORNING, a bang at the door startled them as they sipped tea. Shen motioned for Mac to stay back as he answered the knock.

A tall, bald man wearing several layers of robes that made him appear heavy pushed his way into the room. His voice was loud and blustery. He smelled like dirty socks that had been balled up for a month. Shen remained serene as though someone were telling him a tale. Mac did not understand their conversation.

Shen faced Mac. "He wants to know why you are here. I have explained to him that you are ill and need rest."

"You can tell that smelly ogre I'm leaving today."

"He wants money for lodging."

"This is your house. Why does he get paid and not you?"

"It is his way."

"Well, it's not mine. Tell him not a single yuan."

The intruder made a move on Mac who was ready to defend himself, but before he could react, the extortionist dropped to the floor. Shen had swatted him with his stick to the back of his legs and then bopped him over the head. He lay unconscious.

"I thought you were a pacifist."

"One must be mindful of violence, but in some instances it comes in handy."

Mac saw a smidgen of a smile cross Shen's face. "You're amazing," he laughed.

"You best leave before he wakes. A man outside will show you the way to Chungking."

"Good bye, Shen." Mac bowed. "I hope we meet again."

"Remember, your bones can waste away from guilt. You must first forgive yourself, then seek forgiveness from those you have caused pain." Shen placed a hand on his shoulder as if to bless him. "Find your way to inner peace, my son."

Every muscle in Mac's body relaxed and the fog in his mind cleared something he had not experienced since childhood. He walked away in hopes he could hold on to it.

SIXTEEN
Anya

Why do the gypsies want Joe? Anya thought. His refusal to tell her the truth earlier had her questioning his loyalty. She had a momentary thought of leaving him with them but regained her senses. *After all, he was looking out for my best interest.*

"I'm sorry Nadira, but Joe works with me and under my government's protection."

The old woman marched up to Anya and fixed her face within inches. "There is no government here." She grabbed Joe's arm. "This is no man's country."

He struggled to free himself. "I told you not to trust them."

"We need new blood. My daughter is of marriageable age and needs a husband."

Boy, has she dialed into the wrong number.

The men inched towards Joe. Anya was too far away from her gun to enforce her will. She had to think and think fast.

"It's time for you to leave," the gypsy woman said.

"I can't go without him."

The men encircled her. The eldest pulled out a club from behind his back and slapped it against his palm. "Then you will die."

Anya stepped back. The dog lowered its head, showed its teeth, and snarled. Anya put her hands in front, palms facing the dog. "Okay. No need to get violent. I'm going."

"Anya, you can't leave me." The blub in Joe's voice almost brought her to tears.

She spoke to him in English, knowing the Luoli would not understand. "I'll be back. Be ready." Joe's distraught face made it hard for her to leave, but she vowed to return.

The men and dog were poised to strike as she climbed onto the buckboard. She picked up the reins and nudged the horse to advance. It plotted back down the path from where they had come.

The old woman screamed, "We'd better not see you again."

"Yeah. Yeah. Yeah," she muttered. "Go choke on a fishbone, ya old hag."

Anya arrived at the main road with enough

daylight left to make it back to the campsite before dark. She hid the wagon amongst tall shrubs and weeds and tethered the horse to a tree.

She patted the horse's hindquarters as it grazed. "I'll be back."

She placed one fully loaded Beretta at the small of her back and carried the rifle. *A gun is a good equalizer and two are even better.*

Tired but eager to rescue Joe, Anya advanced. She maintained a safe distance from the glow of the gypsy's campfire. *Now to find Joe.* She crept closer. In front of a plain planked-wood vardo wagon, a man sat on a step with a rifle in hand. *Sentry, um. Now, where's that damn dog?* Anya surveyed the area with no luck. *I'll have to take my chances and stay downwind.*

She snuck to the back of the vardo, picked up a few pebbles, and threw them at the window. She tossed pebbles until she saw the curtain flutter. Peering from behind was Joe. Anya stepped out into the clearing. From inside the wagon, she heard the dog bark and retreated for cover.

A commotion on the other side of the wagon caused her to investigate. The gypsies were setting up what she feared was a marriage canopy. *Don't worry Joe. I'll get you out of this.*

"Anya. Anya."

She returned to the window. "Joe, can you squeeze through there?"

A second person appeared at the window before he could answer. It was Nadira. Anya's heart raced as she raised her weapon.

"Not to worry," Joe said. "She doesn't want to marry me either. She loves a man her father refuses to accept. She wants to help us."

Joe tried to calm the dog. The tenor in his voice changed from gentle pleas to rage.

Anya made her way back for cover but stopped in her tracks when she heard a man's deep voice. "You were told not to return."

"And I told you I was not leaving without him." She turned, her rifle drawn, pointing at the gypsies most vulnerable spot.

He pulled his lips back over his teeth. "You any good with that?"

"Only one way to find out." She motioned for him to move and followed him to the center of camp. Raised voices filled the camp as the others huddled around.

"Joe," Anya yelled. "Come out and leave that mutt inside."

The door creaked open. Joe descended the steps with Nadira. The old woman shrieked when she saw Anya. "We should have killed her."

"Relax, ya crazy coot. I'm only here for Joe." "We are leaving. I don't want any heroes. Got it?" Everyone stood still. Anya fired at the eldest man's feet. "Got it?" Heads nodded except for the one man. She aimed the gun in his direction. He glared at her.

Anya stepped back to leave and lost her footing on a stone. She fell back two steps, arms flailed. She dropped the rifle. The men lunged forward. She steadied herself, reached for the pistol nestled at the small of her back and fired off a shot. It hit the nearest man. He grabbed his shoulder and fell.

The others froze.

A woman wailed, "You've killed him."

"He'll live." Anya controlled the quiver in her voice. "I wouldn't try that again. I have plenty of bullets." Her heart pounded. She hoped her bluff was enough. She was uncertain if she could take them all.

"Joe, pick up the rifle and start down the dirt road."

Anya walked backwards with her eyes on the gypsies. Once they were out of sight, she turned and they both ran.

"They'll be after us. We can outrun them, except the dog," Joe said. "Maybe we can throw them off the track. Head for the trees."

"My kingdom… for a horse," Anya said half-breathless.

"What?"

"Nothing."

"What we need is to confuse the dog." Joe stood still and put his hand to his ear. "I hear rushing water." He headed towards the sound and found a creek down an embankment.

"Wade through it. The dog will lose our scent, and we can catch our breath," he said.

The first plunge of icy cold water sent a throb through Anya's body that felt as though her heart had skipped a beat. "Oh my God. They'll hear my teeth chatter."

The roar of voices and the bark of a dog grew nearer. The stream was not deep enough for them to submerge and hide. Instead, they crouched in the water behind a thicket of cattails. A mob of gypsies stopped at the edge of the water. The dog's nose was to the ground. One man crossed the steam and urged the others. They left the dog to sniff around in circles.

Nadira caught up to the dog. She held a torch and looked in their direction. Anya was sure she had spotted them. She crossed the stream and urged the dog to follow.

Anya and Joe climbed out of the water and made their way back to the road. The sun had set but enough twilight remained for them to find the wagon. The whinny from the horse helped. "Poor thing. He's most likely scared."

A rustle from the bushes caused Anya to spin

around on her heels. She drew her gun and pointed it in the direction of the sound. She cocked the hammer ready to fire. A black face emerged, but before she could fire, Joe pushed her arm away.

"What the hell."

The dog came out with its tail wagging and what appeared to be a smile across its lips.

"I didn't want you to shoot him. He's a friend. I think he wants to join us."

"Sure, why not." Anya stepped onto the buckboard and sat. "As if we don't have enough problems, let's add a dog to the mix."

The dog jumped between the two of them and plopped down. "I call him Hei-Hei," Joe said.

"How befitting, after all, his fur is black." She sensed someone in the shadows and looked around, but saw only darkness. She slapped the reins. "Get going horse. We need to make up lost time."

SEVENTEEN
Mac

MAC EXITED SHEN'S HOUSE. A MAN DRESSED IN A muddy brown hooded robe with a rope tied around his waist hailed him with an uplifted hand. Shen's man led him to the river where they boarded a two-man sampan. The trip would be without conversation, as Shen's man did not speak English. He paddled the boat up river as Mac relaxed in his seat and took in the sights. A touch of fog shrouded the tops of the cityscape of Chungking.

Mac mulled over what he and Shen had discussed. He relished what little peace of mind he had obtained and wanted to preserve it. After this mission, he would try to reconnect with his family, if they would have him. He was certain he had experienced enough adventure for one lifetime.

The guide skirted in and out of traffic; junks,

Nationalists gunboats, and steamboats all vying for position on the river as they neared the city. The guide finessed his way to shore without incident. A row of homes on stilts precariously dotted the hillside. On the plateau hundreds of buildings jetted towards the sky. He did not relish the arduous climb he faced. Where Shanghai resided at sea level, the heart of Chungking rested atop a high hill that stretched for miles. He calculated the climb at about twice the length of a football field. Joy did not enter his thoughts as he faced the hundreds of stairs before him. Peasants labored the climb with various bundles strapped to their backs.

The guide climbed out of the boat and approached a group of men who stood next to odd forms of transportation. A frail young man approached, almost accosted, the guide. The two spoke and then the guide gestured for Mac to follow. Without a word, the guide bowed to Mac and returned to his sampan.

"We take you," the frail man said.

"American Embassy?" Mac said.

"Yes. Sit please." He pointed to a bamboo chair attached to wood flooring with a makeshift flat roof overhead. Two long poles stretched beyond the length of the chair. One man stood at the front between the two poles while the other stood in back. Mac stepped in and sat. He grabbed a cross bar attached to the roof to prevent falling out as they lifted him off the ground.

They navigated up the slimy steps from the mist. Electrical wires crisscrossed overhead between the shanty hovels that lined the walkway. An elderly woman leaned out her window and draped laundry over a line. Several men in tattered clothes carried large water jugs that hung from straps across their shoulders. He heard their disgruntled grunts as they mounted each stair.

Mac passed a shop with a large sign in English that read Chop Suey. Above the door in large print, read, Fried Shrimp and stationed next to it hung a faded red Coca-Cola sign. A couple of American soldiers enter the shop. He assumed they must be with General Joseph Stillwell's unit. Vinegar Joe headed up tactical forces between the U.S. and China.

Ahead, along the side of the steps, a peddler crouched over an open flame. He had over a dozen rat bodies tied together with thick twine that hung off his arm. He grinned up at Mac and offered him a roasted rat. Mac cringed then thought, I'd rather see that thing dead than alive.

Mac breathed a heavy sigh when they reached the top. The jostling from the uneven steps and the rats had made his stomach queasy.

Mac noted that there were no Japanese soldiers,

however, there was a strong presence of Chinese police and military. Unlike Shanghai, the people strolled rather than scurried, smiled rather than scowled with raised rather than lowered heads.

The center of the city bustled with hundreds of rickshaws, bicycles, and autos. Although a modern city, not a single block had all its buildings intact. One or two walls were all that remained of many structures, victim of Japanese bombing raids. Continual road construction prevented anyone from arriving at their destination without crisscrossing the city.

A mob swarmed around two men who argued in the street. A bike lay crumpled on the ground. A rickshaw balanced on top of it. Mac smiled to himself and remembered the Shanghailander squabbles he had witnessed. His smile faded when he recognized a face in the crowd. One bearer lost his footing and the chair tipped to the side. Mac grabbed both bars. Once upright, he searched the steam of people to find the familiar face without success. *I must be seeing things. He's dead.*

"We here," the bearer said as they set Mac down.

Mac reached into his pocket, pulled out his wallet, and handed him a yuan. The men's eyes widened, and together both men bowed low and thanked him.

Mac studied the building. *Where is the U.S. emblem and flag?* He shrugged, walked to the front door and opened it without knocking. A uniformed Marine guard immediately addressed him.

"Your business, Sir?" The guard drew back and scrunched his nose.

"Commander Benson. I need to see the Ambassador—now."

"One moment, Sir." The Marine picked up a phone, dialed a number, and whispered a few words then hung up. "Someone will be with you in a moment, Sir."

The click-clack of heels echoed from down the hall. A boyish-faced blond man who looked as if he were right out of college appeared. He wore a tailored dark blue suit. His brow had a permanent furrow that caused him to appear as though the weight of the world were on his shoulders.

He stretched out his hand then pulled it back and coughed into his hand. "I am Luther Stahl, Assistant to the Ambassador." He did not offer his hand again. "How can I help you?"

"Mac Benson. I am here on urgent business and need to speak with the Ambassador."

Stahl pulled out a white handkerchief with the embroidered initials L.S. and wiped his nose. "Commander Benson. We've been expecting you."

Mac furrowed his brow and shifted his stance.

"The Ambassador is out of the country, but we should talk." He rubbed his nose. "Before we begin, maybe you want to freshen up. We have an excellent bath facility. I think we can find you some clean clothes and scrape up something to eat."

Mac looked at his soiled, tattered shirt and trousers. He rubbed the stubble that seemed more of a beard now and noticed the dirt under his fingernails. He imagined he smelled, but he could no longer detect the stench.

"HAVE A SEAT, Commander Benson." Stahl directed Mac to a high-back wood chair. He sniffed and wiped his nose. "Can't seem to get rid of this cold in all this rain we've had lately."

Mac sat back and crossed his legs. The room seemed large in comparison to the lack of furniture; a couple of mismatched chairs faced an oak desk. No pictures decorated the walls. Mac noted how small Stahl appeared behind the desk. It was not his office, Mac thought. "Thanks for the shower and shave. I didn't realize how much I needed it."

"Glad to oblige. Sorry we couldn't do more. The embassy got bombed out last year. We are in temporary quarters."

Mac shrugged. "It's wartime."

"Can I offer you a drink?"

"Whiskey, neat."

Luther rose and ambled over to a piece of furniture that looked like a radio. The lid lifted and two doors swung open to showcase a full bar.

"Small comforts from home." Stahl removed a crystal decanter and two glasses. He poured two fingers of whiskey into each glass. He handed Mac a glass and returned to his seat.

"I don't really understand why you are in China, Commander." Stahl took a sip.

"What is this, an interrogation?" Mac downed a mouthful.

Stahl cleared his throat and hunched forward. "We've been in communication with Honolulu. Mr. Atwater. I believe you know him."

Mac nodded.

Stahl drew a sheet of paper from a folder. "Atwater has asked us to inform you of a change."

He read from the message. "Utmost importance. Shanghai mission terminated. Agent to return. Signed, Edmund Atwater, OWI." He slid the paper across the desk.

Mac sat frozen, uncertain as to why Atwater, not Donovan sent the message. *This is not Atwater's concern. I don't take orders from the War Department. This is an OSS operation.*

Stahl said, "We can get you on a flight at the end of the week."

Mac leaned forward and glared at Stahl. "I don't

think so." He took a final swig and slammed the empty glass on the desk.

'We're on the same side, Commander."

"Tell that to the late Sheldon Henderson from the Shanghai Embassy."

Stahl's hand trembled as he moved it under the desk. A second or two later, an armed and oversized Marine entered the room. "I'm afraid we must insist."

EIGHTEEN

Mac

MAC REMAINED COMPOSED IN HIS SEAT AS THE hefty six-foot four, big-nosed Marine stood over him. His uniform was tight across his upper arms and against his thighs. He twisted his neck to the left until it cracked and then to the right—snap. He then laced his fingers and stretched them until they popped. This man did not need an M1 rifle—he was a weapon.

Stahl was a meathead, in Mac's words, and he had no intention of obeying the embassy's request for deportation until he finished his mission. Mac decided to wait for an opportunity to arise and make his move.

Stahl stood up, walked around the oak desk, and stopped beside Mac. "Get up," he said.

Before Mac had a chance to react, a high-pitched sound of an air raid alarm blasted the airwaves.

"Damn," Stahl uttered. "I thought those Japs had given up on this city."

From outside the door heavy footsteps scurried past. Grumbles, blubbers, and shouts echoed.

"We need to get to the basement—now," Stahl said. "Bluto, help our guest."

The Marine grabbed Mac's arm with one hand and hoisted him up from his seat. Stahl led the way with Mac sandwiched between them. He felt the steel rod of a rifle barrel on his back as they walked the empty hall. A lone man sprinted past them and down the stairs.

Mac considered his options. *Two men are manageable. The jarhead presents a challenge.* Stahl descended the first step and Mac took his opportunity. He used the sole of his shoe to kick him in the ass. Stahl somersaulted down the steps. Mac twisted around, grabbed Bluto's gun, kneed him in the groin. Bluto doubled over and Mac used the butt of the rifle to knock him unconscious. He removed the Marine's Remington semi-automatic from his holster and placed it in his coat pocket. He would have preferred a Thompson sub-machine gun.

Once outside, Mac raced along the street and headed to a bombed-out building. He assumed it would not be a target and took cover. A plane's thunderous engine passed overhead and he held his breath. He believed anyone who did not fear the possibility of being blown up was one of two things, stupid or crazy.

The whistling sound of a bomb falling was a bleak reminder of the time he had spent in London during the Blitz. It also sparked the memory of the German spy whose neck he had snapped. His stomach churned as Shen's words that evil consumed his soul echoed in his mind. The bomb exploded and Mac jumped. *Easy, old boy.* Ground troops took counter-measures with anti-aircraft guns. Shells pierced the sky and exploded. Smoke lingered. The smell of gunpowder filled the air. The roar of the marauder faded and the air raid sirens halted moments later.

Mac composed himself and left his hideout. He had gone no more than a few blocks when he ran into the frail young man who had hauled him up the hill earlier. The chair and his partner were nowhere in sight.

"Sir, I help you?" he said.

Mac had not bothered to examine the man earlier. His clean-shaven face exposed a scar that stretched from his left temple across his cheek. His clothes fit tight as if meant for someone else. His hands and bare feet held half the city's dirt. A bamboo hat slung around his neck and off his back.

Smoke billowed up from a cigarette that clung to his lips.

"You don't happen to know the whereabouts of Chiang Kai-shek?" He did not ask about Dai Li.

He bowed. "I know all peoples."

This chance meeting troubled Mac. That, and a coin-sized tattoo on his forearm. *Maybe it's a mark of a drug syndicate like the Green Gang in Shanghai.* Reluctant to hook up with this man, Mac knew he had few options.

"What's your name?" Mac said.

"Xiao-Ping. I speak good English." He took a last puff and flicked the cigarette into the gutter.

Mac paused to consider his situation. "Okay Ping," Mac slapped him on the back, "let's go."

They zigzagged through the thousands of muddled refugees and passed under a multitude of towered scaffolding throughout the reconstructed city. A voice yelled from above. Mac glanced up. A metal bucket dangled above his head. He jumped to the side. The pail crashed to the ground and spilled its liquid contents. A splash hit Mac's trouser leg.

"Bombs, buckets…I'm starting to think I'm jinxed," he said.

"You lucky. You meet me, Ping said.

They reached a tree-lined residential neighborhood. The homes, in a neat row, were an eclectic group of western and eastern architecture. Mac and

Ping climbed the stoop that led to a pale yellow Georgian-style house. Ping banged the doorknocker. A peephole opened, a dark eye stared at them, and then disappeared.

The creak of the door resonated as it opened. A man in a white tunic, black slippers, and a black cap ushered them in.

Ping spoke to the servant, who bowed, then shuffled down the hall. The two followed close behind. Mac entered a simple oriental furnished room. He thought it odd that the style of the house contradicted its interior. Over-sized pillows surrounded a black lacquer table that stood about a foot above the floor. A servant entered with a teapot and small bowls and set them on the table.

"Is this Chiang's residence? Mac said.

"You wait. You see."

An average looking Chinese man dressed in a tailored European-style suit with cropped hair invited them to sit. There were no introductions. One of Mac's knees popped when he lowered himself and fell onto a pillow. He grunted as he maneuvered his long legs under the table and crossed them. The servant poured tea into each small bowl.

Ping and their host exchanged words while Mac sipped his tea. He wondered about the relationship between the tailored man and Ping. *Did he need his permission to help him?*

"What you want with Generalissimo?" Ping turned to Mac.

"I have special orders to deliver a message from the American Director of Strategic Services in Washington DC.," Mac lied.

"Why you not use American help?" Ping said.

Mac readjusted his legs. "Let's just say it's best if they stay out of it."

"He say, Chiang gone to India. Maybe three weeks."

"Nevertheless, I would like to at least leave a message and let him know I am in town and will wait for his return." Mac figured if he could get into the building he might be able to search for Li.

The tailored man nodded to Ping, who then rose. Mac tried to stand, but one leg had gone partially numb. He bowed, thanked the tailored man then hobbled away. A sharp tingle ran down his leg as feeling returned.

Night had fallen when they exited the house.

"I get you place for night," Ping said. "We find Chiang place in morning."

"Thank you." Mac wanted to know about the strange man who knew all peoples. "Ping, are you from Chungking?"

"I from East. Too much guns so I come here."

"The tattoo on your arm, what does it mean?"

"It old. It mean nothing." Ping lowered his head

and covered the scar with his hand.

They arrived in front of a narrow dilapidated building. There were no markings on the door to indicate it was a place for rent. The two of them could barely fit in the lobby. There was no elevator, only a narrow staircase. A bald-headed man with a Foo Manchu mustache and beard that looked like he had stepped out of a Charlie Chan movie sat on the other side of iron bars. Mac threw him a few yuan in exchange for the room key. He gave Ping a few coins then headed up the stairs.

The dingy room held a single bed and table with a washbasin. Several holes in the plastered walls exposed support beams. Mac sighed. *Better than sheltering in the cold, wet night air.* He placed his gun under the pillow then fell on the lumpy mattress and laced his fingers behind his head. "Enjoy your last meal, Li, you bastard. Tomorrow you die."

NINETEEN
Anya

ANYA AND JOE RELAXED ON A JUNK THAT TOOK them up the Yangtze River on their final leg to Chungking. They had sold the cart and horse but kept the dog. The captain said they would reach the city before nightfall. The ship had a high stern with projecting bow that carried three hoisted linen sails. It ferried people as well as goods up and down the river. Also aboard were a family and a scholarly looking woman in a brown tweed suit.

Anya bathed in the warmth of the mid-day sun as they sailed through a narrow gorge. On one side of the river stood cliffs as white as chalk with hordes of carved calligraphy etched into the hillside. A single character stretched over six feet in height.

The woman in tweed sat next to Anya. Her fair skin matched the color of her hair. The bridge of her nose supported horn-rimmed spectacles. She held a notebook close to her chest. "They have been here for hundreds of years." She pointed to the cliff.

"Magnificent." Anya said. "What are those steps along the side?"

"Those are the Water-Stealing Holes." She adjusted her spectacles and cleared her throat. "The story goes that during the Ming Dynasty the dark ruler, Xianzhong, tried to take control of the area. The Emperor discovered his plot and sent forces to shut off the source of water supply to the mountain, giving Xianzhong's army the choice to surrender or die of thirst. This was during a time when no rain fell and it was difficult to get water up the mountain. In order to reach the riverside and obtain water, the army chiseled holes in the cliff and inserted wooden pegs to climb down every night."

"Clever," Anya said.

"Never underestimate man's resolve." Joe paused. "Make that woman."

The tweed woman rose, made her way to another part of the boat, sat near the family, and described the cliffs.

"She must be a schoolmarm." Anya winked.

The gorge widened as they continued to forge up-river against the current. Small huts sporadically dotted the land along the bank. A few women used the water flow to wash clothes while others bathed.

Anya turned up her nose at the murky brown river.

Hei-Hei placed his paws on Joe's lap, nuzzled his hand, and blinked up at him. He stroked the dog's long coarse fur. "Miss Anya, what is the plan once we arrive?"

"I'm hoping the American Embassy can help us."

Joe gave her a sheepish glance.

"What?" she said.

"The assistant there—Luther Stahl. He and I had words last time we spoke."

"What do you mean?"

"When the Japanese interned all Westerners, I tried to get his office to set up transportation for Mr. Shelley and me to leave Shanghai. He was very rude and said we were on our own. I told him if I ever saw him, I'd beat him good."

"And…?"

"Miss Anya, I abhor violence." He stopped petting the dog and fell back in his seat. Hei-Hei whined and jumped down.

"Oh, he'll most likely have forgotten all about it."

"I hope so."

THE TOPS OF BUILDINGS pierced through a layer of fog. Within the next hour, they reached the shores of Chungking. The floating pontoons used as docks were laden with all manner of boats that jockeyed for space.

As they docked, Anya focused on the hundreds of stairs and sighed.

"Not to worry, we can take a sedan-chair," Joe said.

"A what?"

"Come, I'll show you." He waved her on.

Joe hailed two chairs. Anya sat in one and held onto a bar as the two men lifted her. Joe, already seated, chuckled at her. Hei-Hei jumped onto his lap. The unexpected added weight caused the carriers to lose control of the chair. Both Joe and the dog tumbled to the ground. Anya released a loud laugh.

The trip to the embassy allowed Anya to get a glimpse of the city. She was dismayed at the number of buildings that were shattered much like their lives yet they continued to survive through the hardship. Many appeared to be refugees probably fled to Chungking to escape the invasion of their cities, towns, and villages.

They arrived at the American Embassy within an hour. Anya opened her bag to draw out a few yuan to give to the carriers when a figure wearing a large white-faced mask with exaggerated black eyebrows, round pink cheeks, and big red lips knocked her to the ground. Hei-Hei arrived by her side followed by Joe, but the bandit had fled the scene before they got to her.

"What happened?" Joe said.

"I don't know. He blindsided me." She picked herself up and took inventory. "Damn. He got my bag. Nothing of real value, but still."

Joe rubbed his chin. "I wonder?"

"What?"

He gave her a 'you-know-who-look.'

"Sun?" She shook it off. "Too agile."

AN ARMED MARINE STOOD stalwart at the entrance of the embassy. Anya recoiled and said to Joe. "Do we dare approach?"

"You tell me. It's your country."

Anya took a deep breath and marched forward with Joe and Hei-Hei close behind.

"Your business, Madam?" The Marine positioned his rifle across his chest. His eyes narrowed at Joe and the dog.

Anya had to adjust her brain to English. It had been several weeks since she heard anyone speak it. "I. . . that is, we are here to see the ambassador."

"He's not here." The Marine's voice was blunt.

"Then we need to speak to someone who is in charge."

"He's busy."

Joe stepped up and addressed the Marine in

English. "Tell Luther Stahl, Joe, from the Shanghai office is here."

The Marine scrutinized Joe. "Wait here."

"Can't we wait in the lobby?" Anya said. "I'm an American citizen."

The Marine returned a blank stare then motioned them inside. They stood on black and white marble tile as the Marine approached a man in a striped suit behind a desk. He whispered to him and then returned to his outdoor post.

"Don't forget to stand your ground with Stahl," Anya leaned over and whispered.

After a brief phone call by the clerk and a few silent minutes, a man in a blue suit appeared from the hallway. "You son-of-a-bitch. You did make it to Chungking." He put up his fists in a playful manner as if he wished to box Joe.

"Yes, I did." Joe stretched himself to stand taller.

Stahl slapped Joe on the back, which caused Joe to lose his balance.

"I'm Anya Pavlovitch." She extended her hand to Stahl. She wondered about his neck brace and black eye.

Stahl hesitated then accepted the handshake. "Russian? We have a lot of your kind here."

His remark made her cringe. "I was born in Russia, but I am now an American."

"Yes, well, what can I do for the two…" His head tiled down at the dog. "Make that the three of you."

Hei-Hei growled.

"Can we go somewhere more private?" Anya said.

"Maybe the dog can stay with the clerk."

Hei-Hei let out a bark and showed his teeth.

"Okay then, my office it is."

A stalky Marine with a large bulbous nose that looked to have been broken in three places passed them on the way to Stahl's office. Anya wondered how many fights he had lost.

Once everyone had sat including the dog who nestled himself next to Joe, Anya began. "I have been asked by the War Department in Honolulu to locate an American agent."

"It wouldn't happen to be Macdonald Benson?" Stahl said.

Anya rose in her seat wide eyed. "Has he been here?"

"Here and gone."

"Gone? Gone where?"

"Unknown." Stahl's face flushed as he tugged at the neck brace. "There was a bit of an altercation and he escaped. We haven't been able to locate him."

"You arrested him?"

"Not exactly. We were told to detain him. You

see, we also received a message from Honolulu."

How can an embassy with Marine guards fail to keep a man locked up? She rethought. *Well, it is Mac after all.* "Doesn't seem that you can help us so, we'll let you get back to work." She stood up.

"We can offer you a place to freshen up and change to proper attire." Stahl scanned her wardrobe.

She had gotten used to her Chinese tunic and drawstring pants. They were more comfortable than the tucked in blouse and waist cinched trousers she normally wore. "No thank you, we have made other arrangements," she lied.

Anya went to walk out the door when Stahl called out. "You'll keep us informed of your progress?"

"Sure," she lied again.

Once outside Joe said, "Why didn't you ask him about Dai Li's whereabouts?"

"I don't want him to know more than I know. I don't trust that guy. He's too G.I.," she paused. "If they find Mac, they will shoot first, and by then, it'll be too late to ask questions. My plan is to talk Mac down."

"How are we going to find Mac in this big city?" Joe said.

"We aren't—Li is."

"Huh?"

"If we monitor Li's movements, Mac is bound to show up."

"That's using the old noodle." Joe pointed his finger to his temple.

"I thought you abandoned the Hardy Boys jargon."

"It pops out once in a while." He smiled.

"Okay, let's go find Dai Li."

"What about Sun?" Joe said.

A cold sweat formed on Anya's brow and her stomach twisted. She remembered Sun's laugh as he divulged to her how he had killed her parents. The knot in her stomach dissipated, replaced by rage.

"That man's nine lives have expired."

TWENTY
Anya

ANYA SAT UP, DISORIENTED, AND SCANNED THE unfamiliar room. The sun streamed through discolored curtains and highlighted barren walls. There was the bed she had slept in and the other bed Joe lay in with Hei-Hei snuggled next to him. A spark of remembrance returned. They had rented a room in Chungking from a crusty old woman.

"Joe, are you awake?" He remained motionless. She threw her pillow at him.

The dog jumped off the bed and Joe rolled over. "I was having the best dream. I dreamt I was eating spicy fishcakes, hairy crabs with roe tofu, and turtle soup."

Anya laughed. "Not sure if we can arrange that, but there is a morning meal included. Let's hurry and get going before the madam stops serving."

After each had freshened up in the community bathroom, they walked downstairs. A young servant bowed and greeted them.

"Breakfast?" Anya said.

The girl's bony red fingers pointed down the hall. Her waifish appearance made Anya wonder if she was indentured. A pungent whiff hit them as they entered the kitchen. The portly landlady was dressed in a floor-length robe. She stirred a well-used pot.

"Sit," she said.

Anya and Joe sat on stools next to a small wooden table. Plated rice cakes sat in the middle of the table. The landlady flung bowls of congee sprinkled with sliced greens in front of them. She then tossed the pot in the sink and stomped out.

"I don't think she likes the dog." Anya sniffed the rice pottage, picked up her porcelain soupspoon, and took a small bite. It had a bland taste much like cream of wheat.

Joe stuck a couple of rice cakes in his pocket then took a spoonful of mush. "What are you going to do about Sun?"

The mention of his name made her stomach twist. She swallowed her bite before answering. "My eyes are not closed to the fact that he is here, but Mac is our first priority." She paused. "Why do you think Sun is in Chungking?"

Joe shrugged and placed his bowl on the floor for Hei-Hei to finish.

Frustrated that her past once again confronted her, Anya gnashed her teeth. It was inevitable that she and Sun would cross paths but she wanted it on her terms.

Anya pulled a piece of paper from her pocket with the name Guo, an address, and directions scribbled on it. Zang had given her the contact before she left Shinjing. "I hope this guy can help us locate Li," she said. "We'd best get moving."

They combed the streets of Chungking. Anya circled in several directions before she found her bearings.

Chinese soldiers zoomed by in a jeep. It was luck that prevented pedestrian carnage. There were so many solders about, she wondered who was fighting the war.

Anya turned a corner and scowled. A boy in a soiled t-shirt that covered his torso, urinated in the street gutter. It was commonplace to see such occurrences. Mothers cut slits in their toddlers pants so they could squat and defecate when the urge came upon them. Sanitation was a luxury during wartime.

She looked straight ahead and sighed. "More stairs. God, there are a lot of steps in this town."

"That's why they call it the mountain city." Joe directed his sly smile to Hei-Hei. The dog's tongue hung inches from his mouth as he panted.

"Even he's worn-out."

"This is it. Fourth house on the right."

The timber shanty buildings, some tilted, nestled together without a space in between. Anya foresaw if one were to collapse, the entire block would crumble. Those that had windows were open to air the rooms. Across the street, various open vendor stalls sold colorful umbrellas, clothes, and baskets. The smell of urine permeated the air.

Throngs of people jammed the walkway as the three trudged up the hill. People bumped and pushed their way without consideration for others. One passerby shoved Anya aside. She protested and the young ruffian half-turned. He raised his fist and scowled at her. He stood out from the crowd with a white sash wrapped around his head. It had red Chinese characters painted on the front.

Joe intervened. "Let it go, Anya. You don't want to get mixed up with his sort."

She watched as the man in white pushed people aside and marched along. "Who was that?

"Gangster."

Anya reached the house and sought shelter under the overhang of the shack. "I feel like I have been beaten up."

"I know. People don't have a sense of others' space. There are too many of us to worry about

English politeness."

Anya knocked on the door. It vibrated and produced a hollow echo. "I hope I didn't knock it off its hinges." She let out a joking giggle. The door squeaked open and a young barefoot boy with short coarse black hair that stuck out in all directions gave them a blank stare.

"Is Guo here?" Anya said. The sound of footsteps creaked across a wooden floor. The door widened. A man about Joe's age pushed the boy aside. His eyes were set far apart and his nose was flat. A once white, now soiled tunic and pants hung off his body.

"Are you Guo?" The dog sniffed him.

"Yes." He backed away from the dog.

"Zang from Shinjing gave me your name. He said you might help us."

Guo stood motionless as he scrutinized them.

"May we come in?" Anya said.

The main room was small with a ratty rug and a few chairs. A war poster hung from a planked wall. It depicted a man and woman in military uniforms bearing rifles. The words "United We Will Win," displayed in bold print on the bottom.

Within moments, ten men from the back of the hovel entered. They all looked in the same condition as Guo, under-nourished and in no mood for uninvited visitors. A few carried short chains attached to wooden handles. Others had batons tucked in their belts. She wondered if they were gangsters. A slight tremble traveled through Anya's body and moisture gathered on her upper lip. Hei-Hei growled. Joe attempted to calm him.

"These are my patriots," Guo said. There was not a smile among them.

Zang had promised they were trustworthy, but uncertainty filled her. She tried to shake off her trepidation. The dog now calm, she exhaled and took his cue.

"I'm searching for Dai Li. I am hoping you can help me find him."

The men looked at each other wide-eyed.

Guo said, "He is evil. What is your business with him?"

"I'm sorry, I can't tell you." Anya swallowed hard. "But it's very important that I speak with him."

The men mumbled to one another, heads turned every so often and glared at her. Guo held up his hand and the room went silent. "Can't make any promises, but we'll see what we can do. Come back in two days."

Anya placed her hands together and gave Guo a slight bow to show her respect. "Thank you."

They had not gone more than a few steps from Guo's place when Anya stopped. "What are those guys into?"

"Haven't a clue, but they don't seem appear to be opium dealers—too poor."

"I hope we're all singing from the same song sheet." A strange insight swept over her and she spun around.

"What?" Joe said.

"Not sure. I have the feeling someone is watching me." She scraped her top teeth across her bottom lip. "It's probably nothing. I'm just dog-tired."

TWENTY-ONE
Mac

MAC WASHED THE MORNING SLEEP OFF HIS FACE and patted it dry with a towel. He combed his fingers through his hair and put on his coat. The seriousness of the day would prove rewarding or vexing. He picked up the Remington he had confiscated from the Marine. He stepped outside expecting rain. Instead, the air was warm. Ping was leaning against the building smoking.

"Let's go," Mac said.

"It very far to south end." Ping pushed off the wall and stomped out his cigarette on the sidewalk. "We need chair."

Mac remembered his last bumpy ride that made him queasy. "I'd rather walk."

Ping moaned as they headed out.

Near noon, a sweet aroma from an outdoor

market enticed Mac. They passed several food vendors before Mac decided on a pork bun. He felt obliged to buy one for Ping. Mac finished his meal and noticed Ping hovering around a fruit vendor. Ping walked away without making a purchase. He sauntered up to Mac, pulled out two ill-gotten lychee nuts from his pocket, and gave one to Mac. Mac watched as Ping unpeeled the pink-red rind exposing translucent white flesh. He mimicked Ping's actions and bit into the fruit. Its sweet juice helped satisfy his thirst.

An eerie sensation pricked at Mac's spine. A feeling he had not sensed since his days in London. He looked to his left, pretending to scratch his chin on his shoulder. A Chinese man in a dark European suit admired bamboo hats. He appeared out of place. Mac knew in an instant something was awry.

"I need you to run interference with the guy three stalls away," Mac said out of the corner of his mouth. "I'll meet you four blocks south of here."

Ping nodded.

Mac walked faster and faster. He shoved his way through the crowd. He took a hard left and hurtled over a vendor's merchandise. The vendor screamed at Mac and hit him with one of his baskets. The blow threw him off his feet. The vendor continued to pound the basket on his back. He tried to stand, but a hefty wallop pushed him down. He flipped over and used his feet to kick the basket out of his hands. The vendor stood stunned. Mac got up, bowed, and ran.

He spied another man. Bluto. One of Stahl's jarheads from the embassy. He skirted behind a rack of clothes. Bluto grabbed him by the legs and tackled him. They wrestled on the ground while gawkers encircled them. A crowd of ten had formed around them. Little old men placed bets before he took a right hook to the chin. He countered Bluto with the same compliment. Free from his clutches, Mac sprang to his feet. He kicked Bluto in the head and knocked him down. He lay stunned for a moment. The masses erupted with several congratulatory slaps. Money exchanged hands as Mac took off.

Confident he had lost his shadows, he met up with Ping. Short of breath, Mac said, "Tha . . . thanks . . . for the assistance."

"Who that guy?"

Mac brushed himself off. "Somebody who wants me out of town." It occurred to him that he could not trust the American or the Chinese military. Ping was now his only ally.

MAC AND PING ARRIVED at Chiang Kai-Shek's residence late in the afternoon. Streaks of sunlight pierced through parted clouds onto a lush forest that carpeted the large compound. One structure peaked above a grove of trees. A guard stood vigilant at the gated entrance. Tucked away from view, Mac surveyed his options.

"Guard not let you in," Ping said.

"I have no intention of asking permission."

Ping's brow furrowed.

"There's a lot of wooded acreage. They can't possibly monitor every inch," Mac said. "I just need to find the right spot."

Mac circled around to the right and found a suitable place a good distance from the entrance. The roar of an engine from the other side of the fence stopped them in their tracks. Hunkered down, they watched as two soldiers, a rifle visible in the hand of the passenger, careened by in a jeep. Once it was out of sight, Mac made his move.

"This is where I leave you, Ping."

"I go too."

"It's too dangerous."

"I no afraid." Ping held his breath.

"Okay." Mac flagged him forward.

Ping exhaled with a smile that stretched across his face.

Mac climbed the wire fence. "I hope they don't use dogs." He threw his coat over the barbwire at the top and maneuvered over. Ping followed his lead. His foot twisted between the wires. In his struggle to free himself, his other foot slipped and he fell backwards. The one thing that saved him from hitting the ground was his snared foot as he dangled upside down.

"Christ," Mac mumbled as he jumped to the ground. "Grab onto the wire and pull yourself up."

Ping reached for the wire, first one hand and then the other. He managed to right himself.

"Free your foot and climb over. Hurry up, man."

Ping stood next to Mac. "That close call."

Mac patted him on the back then they raced into the forest of trees. They passed a single story brick house a few yards ahead. Music in the distance captured Mac's attention. Together, they crept toward the sound. In a clearing, large stone steps led to a grassy area surrounded by tall thin trees with long finger-like branches that almost touched the ground. A woman sat on a stone bench with a cigarette in her hand and hummed. White butterflies fluttered behind her. Her pinned back dark wavy hair and erect posture gave her an air of elegance.

"Madame Chiang," Ping whispered. "She must hide smoke. No good for woman to show."

"We'd best press on before we're discovered."

A loud crack echoed when Ping stepped on a fallen branch.

She rose from her seat. "Is someone there?"

Mac placed his finger to his lips and cautioned

Ping to remain quiet. The back of Mac's neck bristled. Her eyes seemed to pinpoint their location. She moved in their direction. A voice from above called to her. She stopped. The voice rang out again. She stamped out her cigarette and walked up the steps to the house. Ping exhaled and wiped his brow with the back of his hand. Mac waved him on.

They crept along the wooded path until they came upon a building in the clearing. It had contemporary features much like a three-story rectangle with a multitude of windows stacked vertically and horizontally. Other than two lanterns suspended on either side of the entrance, it resembled an office building in any American city.

The sky had turned dark and cold. Wet fog had settled in. Mac had to find shelter. After a half-hour of searching, they stumbled upon a storage shack. They would hole up until daylight.

Ping's stomach grumbled. "I hungry."

"Yea." Mac placed a hand on his belly.

"I go find food."

"Be careful."

Mac entered the shed and groped around in the dark. He stepped on a rake that smacked him square in the face. "Damn it." He rubbed his nose and envisioned his next move. *Killing Li may take a minimal effort, but escaping will be tricky.* The cautionary words from Mathew, Shen, and Anya rattled in his mind. *I will pray for your soul. It is honorable to keep your word, as long as it does not consume the goodness. You must survive for the sake of your wife and daughter.* He shook his head to erase their words. "Honor, country and duty" he repeated several times.

Ping returned in an hour with partially eaten fruit and half a sandwich. "Trash good place for food."

Ping held his hands out. Mac selected an apple with a single bite missing. Not sure when his next meal might be, he wiped the apple on his sleeve then took a bite from the opposite side.

Mac sat upright and leaned against a bag of dirt. He finished the apple then closed his eyes and thought about what tomorrow would bring.

MAC AROSE BEFORE THE SUN and had returned to his hiding spot in front of the office building. He believed it was the best angle to encounter Dai Li. He craved a hot cup of coffee as he crouched in the bushes. The musty aroma of damp foliage flooded his nostrils. He had reconsidered his plan. Instead of eliminating Li here and finding certain death, he decided to tail him and wait for a more opportune time.

Mac watched a uniformed man walk up to the front door, unlock it, then switch on the lobby lights. He positioned himself behind a desk at the center of the room. Men and women trailed into the building. Some wore traditional Chinese attire, a few sported Western suits. Within seconds, lights from various offices flipped on.

Mac jumped when Ping made a sudden appearance.

"Where have you been?" Mac said.

"I talk to cook. She say Li be here lunchtime, maybe."

"What?" Mac scowled at Ping.

"No worry, cook relative."

"Did you get any food?"

Ping grinned and held out a bag filled with dumplings.

IT WAS WELL PAST NOON when fatigue and restlessness set in. Mac was more than anxious to end this assignment. But in another vein, he dreamed about the accolades and possible promotion from the success of this mission. *Let's not get ahead of ourselves, old boy.*

A shiny black sedan drove up and parked at the building entrance. The chauffeur opened the back door of the car and a man exited. Mac had long since lost the black and white photo of Li. The receded hairline and flat nose appeared the same, but something about the ears did not ring true. It all pointed to Dai Li, yet something familiar about the man haunted him. Mac was not close enough for visual confirmation, but he did not care. His adrenaline surged. His logic took flight. He went for his gun.

TWENTY-TWO

Anya

ANYA FIDGETED WITH HER RING FINGER AND paced the room, anxious for the news Guo would bring regarding Li the following day. She thought about how she would approach Mac but quickly cleared her mind. Today demanded little attention to her mission. She decided to distract herself by exploring the city.

She, Joe, and Hei-Hei passed under a pagoda archway designed with various triangular shaped red and blue tiles that decorated the wing-roof structure. A market plaza revealed itself on the other side of the threshold. Hordes of people crowded around rows of neatly lined vendors.

They passed a feeble old man who sat cross-legged on the ground with a bow and played a stringed musical instrument that emanated a high-pitched tone. It had a long thin neck. The top held two tuning pegs. At the bottom was a sound box covered in a tanned animal skin. He played it like a vertical violin. It reminded her of the sounds she had heard when she walked through San Francisco's Chinatown.

Ahead, loud squawks drew their attention. Anya and Joe approached stacks of small cages crammed with live hens and chicks for sale. The stench of a barnyard hit their noses hard. Anya turned and stopped cold. She gasped and covered her mouth. In one of the booths, butcher hooks pierced through the jaws of suspended dead dogs.

Joe positioned Hei-Hei close to him. "Men eat dog in the winter," he said. "They believe it keeps them more virile." He nudged her forward as they continued to make their way among the crowd.

Similar to Dorothy when she first saw Oz, Anya soaked in vibrant colors of red, yellow, and orange. Large wooden bowls spread across a long table contained garlic, chilies, and other varieties of colorful spices. The aromatics were a welcome change. Barbecue stations served chicken, pork, and various red meats with their own delicious scents. Anya wondered if dog meat was in the mix.

"Miss Anya, what if we cook for our host tonight?"

"Why would you suggest such a thing?"

"I don't think I can eat any more of Madame's meals. My intestines feel like they are about to explode."

Anya rubbed her belly. "I know what you mean."

They gathered garlic and onions from one vendor, carrots and celery from another, and greens from yet another. Joe picked out chilies, cinnamon, nutmeg, cloves, and fennel seed while Anya bartered for a chicken that hung in a different booth. For the first time in months, her body was relaxed. Her mind did not occupy espionage or pursuance or murder. That all ended when she heard a scuffle several booths ahead.

By the time they made their way to the commotion, the crowd had disbursed. All that remained was a man who lay unconscious on the ground. Anya tilted her head for a better inspection. In a second, she recognized the bulbous broken nose. He had passed her in the hall at the American embassy. *Looks like he's lost another fight.*

Her head jerked up and with widened eyes she said, "Mac's been here."

Anya took a step back and bumped into someone. Out of habit, she turned to apologize. The blood washed from her face. Her heart began to race. A tremble surged throughout her body. She tried to speak but sound failed her. The man who killed her parents. The man who tried to kill her. The man who she believed was dead. There stood Sun Temujin.

His thick, coarse black hair lay under a black cap with a red dragon design stitched on the front. His eyes resembled dark gashes, and a gruesome scar tore across his forehead. He wore an oriental frock, not his traditional double-breasted suit. His constant cane was absent replaced by something in his hand.

"How . . . how did you survive?" Anya said.

He gave her a grin that twisted her stomach.

"You left me for dead." He sneered. "You can't kill me. I'm invincible."

The urge to seize his throat overwhelmed Anya, but her legs failed her. She sensed Joe and Hei-Hei next to her and regained her composure.

"I would have died had you not forgotten one thing," Sun said.

Anya studied his physique. Sun seemed older—frail—vulnerable. Nevertheless, his mercenary background made her wary.

"You forgot about my man you forced into the water closet."

Anya had a vague recollection of a timid man who had agreed to lock himself in the train compartment while she held a gun on Sun.

"He told the Japanese soldiers we'd been taken prisoner and that I was dead. He then took me to a doctor who stitched me up, and with my servant's blood resurrected me. So here I am, ready to regain what is mine and inflict a little sweet revenge."

"You seek revenge?" Anya said. "You are . . ." foam passed her lips, ". . . the most contemptible, vile creature in this universe."

"I want the ring back. I assume it's on your body since I didn't find it in the bag." Sun made a move that caused the dog to lurch forward. Joe grabbed Hei-Hei as Sun stepped back.

"It was you in the white mask?" Joe said.

"Not me, but a sniveling creature I hired." He twirled the string of the mask around his index finger.

"Nothing on earth would compel me to give up my ring." Anya hugged the bags of food close to her chest where she had secured it.

"We shall see." He smiled.

Both were at a standoff. She with an armful of groceries and he without the means to strike out for fear the dog might attack. Sun retreated. She waited until he became lost in the stream of people before she allowed herself to walk away.

Once out of sight, she exhaled. "Well, now we know why he is here." She patted Hei-Hei. "Thanks, buddy."

ANYA LAY IN HER BED that evening and recalled the day. Madame had been delighted to receive the food but insisted on cooking. She and Joe watched her prepare the meal to ensure that she used the items they had purchased. Similar to a seasoned butcher, the Madame wheeled a cleaver and chopped the chicken into pieces. Anya had wondered where Madame's husband was since they never saw him.

Madam had pulled out a tarnished wok with generations of use and set it over an open flame on the stove. She tossed in diced vegetables and spices, then used a flat metal spatula with a shovel shape and pushed the food about like a choreographed dance. Maneuvering the meal up the deep side of the wok, she then added the rice and broth. After several minutes, she stirred the mixture together, then served it on a platter, and laid it in front of them.

Although supper was good, Anya had not eaten much. Restless, she rose from her bed, wrapped the blanket around her, and walked to the window. The dog lifted its head then lay back down while Joe slept.

She stared out at the fog that nestled over the city lights reminiscent of San Francisco, albeit absent of foghorns. *How deceptively serene things appear at night. I can't believe we were all in the same place on the same day at exactly the same time.* She pushed her hair from front to back and sighed. *I hate to think what our next meeting will encompass.* She felt as insignificant as a droplet of rain. She secured the blanket tight across her shoulders. "Mac, wherever you are, I hope you are safe tonight."

TWENTY-THREE
Anya

ANYA AND JOE STEPPED OUT INTO A CHILLY, partially cloudy, morning. They left Hei-Hei with the landlady, under the provision that payment would be forthcoming, and headed for Guo's place. Anya twisted her naked ring finger, anxious to learn the location of Dai Li. Stahl was another worry. He may have figured things out and planned to ambush Mac. Her hopes rested on her finding him before Stahl.

A cavalcade of American jeeps roared past. American forces in Chungking were no surprise. She had seen G.I.'s dole out candy bars to street children upon their arrival. Anya also knew General Stillwell had been charged to build a supply road from India to western China. They continued to snake through the streets heeding road and building repairs underway.

A toothless boy greeted them when they arrived at the house. He pointed up the hill and said his father would meet them at the noodle shop. Anya thanked him and trudged up the steps.

Out of breath at the top, Guo and a few of his friends met them outside of the shop. From their stance and the grim look on their faces, something seemed amiss. She half-turned to see several men march towards them. They wore white tunics and pants and white headbands with large red characters painted on them. The same uniform as the rude man she had encountered the previous day.

"What's going on?" Anya said.

"Rival gang—the White Tigers," Guo said. "They deal in drugs and prostitution. They want to expand and bring their filth into our territory."

A slight smile crossed Anya's face and she laid her right hand over her heart. She had believed he and his gang were the bad guys. Shame washed over her for her prejudice.

"You two best stand clear," Guo said.

His words were still in her head as long sticks, chains, and clubs unfolded. She said to Joe, "In America, the gangsters use Tommy guns to settle their arguments."

Shouted threats and obscenities filled the air. The other gang struck first. A raised leg and heel drove near one of Guo's men. He reacted with an arm block and returned a kick to the groin. The rival man hit the ground with a loud moan. Guo's man finished him off with a stomp to the neck. Another attacker lifted his right knee to his chest and kicked out like a mule. Quick hand movements collided together with various blocks. Clubs clunked. Chains clanked. Bones snapped.

The fast action made Anya dizzy. She found it difficult to determine where one fight started and another ended. Her back to the wall, she picked up a forgotten bat for protection. She hit anyone over the head who approached her dressed in white. One assailant came straight at her. She jammed the end of the bat into his belly. He bent over and she clobbered him.

Joe got in a few kicks. He used the heel of his fist to strike the bridge of an opponent's nose which caused the gangster to clutch his face and bend forward. Joe then swung his arm in an axe-like motion to the neck. The gangster collapsed. Joe quickly regained his stance to prepare for the next attack. She was amazed at his hidden talent and wondered why he had not used it when Guy had brutalized him for information about Mac or at the gypsy camp.

Anya turned as Guo fell to his knees. She did not hesitate before she advanced with club in hand. Anya swung the formidable weapon like Babe Ruth.

The thud against the perpetrators back ricocheted through her arms. Guo bounced to his feet and gave Anya an appreciative bow.

Anya swung her stick and accidently knocked out one of Guo's men. She bit her lower lip, then apologetically shrugged her shoulders at Guo.

"He's better off unconscious. More fighting skills required for that one," he said.

A man in white marched towards her. She held her club tight. An expressionless look on his face made her hesitate. In the next moment, his eyes crossed and he fell forward. In his place, stood one of Guo's men. He smiled and bowed. The fight lasted a few more minutes before those in the repugnant gang still able to flee, vanished.

Joe ran up to Anya and tapped her on the shoulder. "That was fantastic."

"You were amazing," she said. "Where did you learn those moves?"

"My uncle tired of me coming home with bumps and bruises as a boy. He insisted I learn how to fend for myself. I use it when necessary."

They looked at each other and said in unison, "It was necessary."

Guo sidled next to them. "The streets are safe for now, but they will continue to come at us until they get their way. Our job is to see that they don't succeed."

"Guo," Anya said. "I need Li's whereabouts. Do you have anything for me?"

"I can do one better." He waved over one of his men. "This man will take you to him. Thank you for your assistance today. We shall never forget you." Guo extended his hand.

"It's nice to know we are both on the same side." She accepted his handshake.

IT WAS LATE IN the afternoon when they approached the compound. Exhausted, she wanted to wait until tomorrow to speak to Li but reconsidered in case Stahl or Mac got there first.

The rifle-bearing guard at the gate gave Anya pause. Guo's man stepped forward and whispered into his ear. The guard nodded.

"I must leave you," Guo's man said. "Continue on the path and it will lead you to a large building. Inside you will find Li."

"How were you able to get us in?" Anya said.

"The guard, he is my cousin." He winked and walked away.

They turned and headed up the tree-lined paved road, walking parallel on a dirt path.

Joe pushed his hands into his pants pockets. "I wish we had Hei-Hei."

"They might not have let us pass with a dog."

"Still . . ."

They had not walked far when a black Rolls-Royce pulled over. Anya recognized the Flying Lady hood ornament. The back seat window rolled down and a man peeked out.

"Would you care for a ride?" he said.

Anya could not help but notice his large ears that stuck out like devil's horns. His crisp attire looked as if it had come straight from the laundry.

Joe nudged her.

Anya ignored him. "Do you still think we'd have had an offer for a ride with a dog?" She muttered as she entered the vehicle.

Joe remained hesitant until she flagged him to enter. The back seat was roomy enough for all three to fit comfortably.

Without introduction, the big-eared man said, "What brings you here?"

Anya took notice of the big-eared man's custom-made western style suit that fit his slim frame perfectly. He wore silk socks and smart pointed European boots. She glanced around for a top-hat, instead spotted a black bowler. She said, "I seek a man."

"About?"

She felt Joe elbow her in her side. She remained coy. "Official business."

"I see. I'm an official, maybe I can help you."

"Well…it's about…"

Joe again jabbed her.

"What type of business?"

"It's personal. I can't really discuss it." Anya fidgeted with her top blouse button. The stare in his black eyes made her nervous. She questioned if she had said too much.

The road led to an open courtyard. A three-story, modern office building stood at the end of the circular driveway. The car veered around and stopped in front. The driver jumped out of the car and opened the passenger door. The Chinese man emerged followed by Anya then Joe.

Anya thanked him and proceeded to the building. He did not accompany them, instead stayed with the car as they walked up the stairs.

"Why did you elbow me in the car?" Anya said.

"Don't you know who that is?"

"No. But I assumed it wasn't Li, he didn't wear a uniform."

Joe took a deep breath and gulped it down.

TWENTY-FOUR
Mac

MAC HUNKERED DOWN BEHIND BRUSH AND TALL weeds with enough visibility to see the chauffeur scurry to open the car door. A thin Chinese man of average height emerged from the black sedan. There was a familiarity about him. Maybe due to his photo. Maybe due to the hunt. Maybe he just wanted it to be him. Mac's heartbeat remained steady. However, beads of sweat on his upper lip and the perspiration from his palm had loosened his grip on the pistol. His arduous journey through torture, disease, and imprisonment in his pursuit of this man had arrived.

At last, we meet, Dai Li. Mac wrapped his fingers tight around the back strap of the pistol and stood up. Ready to take action and reveal himself, he paused. A woman exited the car. Mac froze. His mind went blank and then snapped to attention.

"What the bloody hell…"Mac squatted down. Ping crouched next to him. "What wrong?"

"She went home, so I thought." Mac said.

Anya smiled and shook the big-eared man's hand as though they were old friends. *Was this another one of her half-cocked schemes like those that got me into trouble back in Shanghai?*

"You know woman?"

Mac ground his teeth. "Unfortunately."

Joe descended from the car. He wiped the palm of his hand across the side of his head. "Christ. I suppose Bia and her husband will be next."

"Who?"

"Never mind," Mac muttered. He watched Anya and Joe stop and talk for a moment before they entered the office building. *What is she doing here?* They entered the building and spoke to the lobby guard.

Mac's eyes shifted back to the car. He did not have a clear visual of the man's face, but the hunt for this man and all it entailed swelled up in him. All reason and discretion vanished. He rose, wrapped his finger around the trigger, and advanced. He wanted to see his eyes. He did not intend to shoot him in the back—that would be cowardly. A firm grip on his forearm halted him.

"That not Li," Ping whispered.

"What are you talking about?"

"Blue, blue, blue." Ping tugged at Mac's shirt.

Mac recalled Li's photo he had seen back at OSS headquarters. The black and white image did not reveal the color of his uniform. He remembered that Li was a member of the Blue Shirts Society. A lawless band Li commanded whose purpose was to thwart the Communists and Japanese puppet organizations in China.

"Well then, who the hell is he?"

Ping shrugged.

"This certainly presents a new wrinkle." He secured the gun at the small of his back. The big-eared man, closer now, turned in Mac's direction. A cold chill ran through his entire body. He had not recognized him without his gown with small monkey heads sewn into the back. It was Du Yu-seng, the man who had ordered him brutalized.

Mac's chest tightened. He rolled forward onto his knees and landed on dry twigs. The loud crackle caused Yu-seng to focus his attention their way. He had no orders to kill Yu-seng, who was in business with Chiang and Li, but he seriously thought about shooting him. However, it would expose himself and thwart his mission.

Mac regained his composure and motioned to Ping to lay prone on the ground. Yu-seng spoke to the driver then walked in their direction. Mac and Ping crawled backwards down a small embankment where they remained motionless. The scent of soil and animal excrement that clung to their clothes circulated. Ping started to sneeze and Mac pushed his face into the ground. The dirt muffled his explosive spasm.

Mac heard footsteps near. He peered through the weeds and watched Yu-seng scan the area. Something caused Yu-seng to turn back and walk away. Mac's ears perked up. The yelp of nearby dogs alerted him to mount an escape plan.

Ping's lips trembled and he started to shake. Mac grabbed him by his shirt and jerked him up. The two ran stooped along the bottom of the gulley. Distant voices swelled alongside Ping's whimpered cries.

The trees thinned exposing the wire fence. Mac made a beeline for it. Ping hesitated at the fence. Mac grabbed him with one hand on the back of his collar and the other hand on his belt. He propelled him onto the barrier as the first of the dogs arrived. The lanky hound lunged at Mac. His quick reflex evaded the dogs attack by moving to the side. The dog crashed into the wire. The momentary stun gave Mac the chance to ascend.

A second hound nipped at his foot as he climbed the fence. He tried to shake it off but it clamped down onto his shoe. Mac heard the rustle from the brush as soldiers closed in on him. He pulled up his leg and loosened the laces as the dog hung on. One lace, then two, and three laces unthreaded. The shoe slowly gave way. The dog and his shoe fell to the ground. Mac scrambled up the fence. Ping had already bounded over and dashed to the other side of the road by the time Mac reached the top. Once over, Mac followed Ping into nearby woods.

Mac glanced over his shoulder. A soldier raised his rifle and aimed his way. He ducked and zigzagged with a bit more speed. He was into the first line of trees when shots rang past his ear. Low hanging tree branches scraped his face and sharp brush tore at his hand. They continued to run until Ping collapsed, out of breath. Mac sat on a log and struggled to catch his breath.

Ping sucked in a breath. "Who that man?"

"The drug lord of Shanghai. A cold-blooded murderer." Mac rested his elbows on his knees, laid his forehead in his hands and tugged at his hair. *I can't believe she is working with Yu-seng.*

He sat upright and stared into the distance. *If she gets in the way…she just better keep her nose out of it.*

TWENTY-FIVE
Anya

ANYA STOPPED AT THE TOP OF THE STAIRS outside Generalissimo's office. She placed her hands on her hips. "Out with it, Joe. Who's the Chinese guy we hitched a ride from?" She glanced down to the driveway where the big-eared man stood. His return stare made her skin prickle.

Joe's cheeks bloomed pink. He cowered slightly. "His name is Du Yu-seng. You know, the boss of the Green Gang back in Shanghai. He…he kidnapped Mac and had Sun torture him." Joe bit down on his index fingernail like a naughty child waiting for punishment.

"Jesus." A revisited vision of Mac hanging by his arms, unconscious, popped into Anya's mind. Her stomach twisted and she massaged her belly. She watched Yu-seng head for the trees. "That makes sense as to why we saw Sun at the market. The two probably traveled here together." She paused. "Yu-seng may not know who we are. Let's keep it that way."

Joe fidgeted with the hem of his tunic. "He may not know you, but remember, he knows my uncle and me." Anya continued to observe Yu-seng and wondered where he was going. "Huh? I wonder why he didn't mention it?" She shook her head. "Can't think about that now, we have more important things." Joe opened the door, and she entered the building with him behind. She dismissed the baying of dogs in the distance as the door closed after them.

A man sat behind a chrome and glass table and gave them the once over. "May I help you?" He held an air of arrogance.

Anya straightened her spine and cleared her throat. Her tenacity tended to emerge when confronted with bad behavior, especially self-appointed importance. "I'm here to see Dai Li."

"He is not here."

"When will he return?"

The lobby guard shrugged.

"Today? Tomorrow? Next week?" Anya said.

"Unknown."

"Well then, who does know?" Her voice hit an octave higher and her face flushed. "I am on official U.S. government business. It's imperative I speak with him."

The guard's eyes widened. He rose to his feet and stood at attention. Footsteps clicked across the linoleum floor. Anya spun around to see Yu-seng approach.

"Maybe I can help?" Yu-seng said. He and the guard exchanged whispered words. The guard picked up the phone and dialed a number.

Yu-seng extended his arm and pointed to a waiting area with several white leather upholstered chairs. "Please have a seat. Someone will assist you shortly." He then exited the building.

"Where is he going? Joe said.

"I don't know." The two observed through the floor-to-ceiling windows as he returned to his car and then sped off. "Perhaps he wanted to see Li too."

Anya fell back into the chair. *If Li is not here, who or what are we waiting for?* She strummed her fingers on the arm of the chair, her knees continually knocking together. She glanced over at the guard who shuffled papers. Every so often, he glanced up at them. Two men, a younger one dressed in a western suit the other older heavyset with a queue in tunic and pants, had come and gone while they waited.

Restless, Anya rose and paced back and forth. She stopped and turned to Joe. "Do you think this is a good idea?"

"What do you mean?"

"Meeting with Dai Li to see if he can help us."

"Sometimes you have to dance with the devil."

"Are those Chinese words of wisdom?" She sat again and reclined. Joe gave her a broad smile.

Anya bolted up in seat. "Did you hear that?"

"No, what?"

"Gunfire."

The guard raised his head and looked out the window. "They use moles as target practice." He returned to his duties.

"I guess that's why they had the dogs," she said.

"Just as long as they don't think we're moles," Joe said.

Out of the corner of her eye, a car fast approached. It was not Yu-seng's. This one was midnight blue with small American flags flapping on the ends of the front bumpers. "Stahl," Anya mumbled. *Yu-seng had the guard call the American Embassy.* Her hands balled up into fists as she sprang to her feet. "I can't believe he had him call that sniffling weirdo."

The chauffeur opened the door and out stepped the ambassador's assistant. They watched Stahl climb the stairs. He withdrew a white handkerchief from his back pocket and wiped his nose as he entered the building. He bypassed the guard and headed straight to the waiting area.

"Please sit, Miss Pavlovitch." Stahl walked to a

chair next to her. When he sat, air rushed out from the cushion and made an embarrassing sound. Joe snickered. Stahl ignored him and continued to wipe his nose. "This damn fog. I can't seem to get rid of this runny nose."

"I like the fog. It reminds me of San Francisco." A moment of melancholy washed over her. Anya imagined she and Paval at the kitchen table sipping vodka and having a laugh. In some way, she wished she could go back in time. *That life has vanished.* She remained in her thoughts until she heard a voice.

"Let's end the masquerade, Miss Pavlovitch." Stahl stuffed the handkerchief in his pocket. "Why are you here to see Dai Li?"

Anya sat with her hands folded in her lap. She stared into Stahl's dark brown eyes. *Do I trust him? No way. Should I tell him the truth? Not all of it.* She let out a sigh. "I… I need to warn Dai Li."

"Warn him? About what?"

Anya rubbed her finger. "His life is in danger."

"What are you talking about?"

"It's true," Joe interjected.

Stahl squinted at Joe. "Stay out of this boy."

Joe's jaw tightened.

"I've been ordered by OWI to find an agent who might try to kill Dai Li."

Stahl rubbed his hairless chin as if to lengthen it. "I see. That answers the question why we received a message to detain Commander Benson."

Anya's body went rigid. She had not counted on Stahl putting the pieces together. "Yes. But I believe I can reason with him to forgo his mission and send him home."

"He seems a very determined man." He sniffed.

"Mac has lost communications with his command and is on his own. He is under orders that no one except he and the man who gave the order know about. Why would he trust you?"

"I see your point."

"I still think there is a chance to resolve this without anyone getting killed."

"I have people who can assist you."

"I prefer to work on my own for now."

"Well, I can't afford to take the chance that this rogue agent is out there ready to destroy our relationship with Peanut by snuffing out his head of security."

Anya wrinkled her brow. "Peanut?"

"That's a nickname Stillwell has bestowed on General Chiang Kai-Shek." Stahl smiled then his smile vanished. "We need to join forces to intercept and stop this man."

"Agreed," Anya said. "Let me try it my way first. If I fail then you can bring in the Marines."

Stahl stood to leave. "Very well, Miss Pavlovitch, but we will be watching."

Anya's eyes followed Stahl as he walked down the stairs to his car. "Joe, we must find Mac."

"How?"

"Exactly. How?" She scratched her head. "We could . . ." She twisted her lips and exhaled, ". . . no, that won't work."

"What if we retrace our tracks?" Joe said. "Go back to the market where you said he clobbered one of Stahl's men."

"Mac wouldn't go back there again. They'd have it staked out." Anya hesitated. "We need a way to sniff him out." She spun around and snapped her fingers. "That dog of yours may earn his keep yet."

TWENTY-SIX
Anya

THE LAST OF THE SUNLIGHT FILTERED BETWEEN dark clouds as night descended. "Looks like rain," Anya said as she and Joe entered their lodgings. She barely had a chance to open the door to their room when Hei-Hei leaped into Joe's arms. He had a piece of paper stuck to his paw. Anya pulled it free. "Most likely a bill for sheltering the dog."

She threw her coat on a nearby chair, pulled off her shoes, and plopped down on her bed. They had been on their feet all day in search of Mac. She placed one arm behind her head and leaned against the pillow. She fanned her face with the note. "I had hoped by now we would have had a clue to Mac's location. We've got to find him before Stahl does."

"What does the note say?" Joe petted Hei-Hei.

Anya unfolded it and began to read. She felt her

cheeks flush as she sat up. "I . . . it . . . as I suspected, it's a bill for the dog care." She folded the paper and placed it in her pants pocket.

"How much?"

"What?"

"How much is it?"

"Don't worry about it. I'll take care of it later." Anya rose from her bed, pulled her hair behind her ears, and paced about the room. "I feel restless. I'm going for a walk." She sat, slipped on her shoes, and picked up her coat.

"Hei-Hei could probably use some exercise. We'll go with you."

"No." Her voice was not her normal tone. "I mean, I need time alone…to think things out." Joes' face expressed puzzlement but the message specifically stated—come alone.

ANYA STEPPED OUTSIDE to a fully engulfed darkened sky. Rain threatened and she was glad she had grabbed an umbrella. Even if it might not be necessary, it could prove to be a formidable weapon. *I'd rather use that than my gun.* Her Beretta was nestled in her right coat pocket.

The crowds bumped her as they passed. She felt their eyes on her as though they knew something. Was it a sign—a warning—an omen. Her inner radar lit up, warry of what lay in wait.

She had gone a few blocks before she stopped and half-turned to assure that Joe had not followed. She fingered the cryptic note in her left pocket. *How did Mac know where we're staying? How did he see us but we missed him?* Wet fog misted over her face. She pulled her coat collar up around her neck and headed to the meeting place.

Anya passed under a three-arched gate adorned with several red lanterns that swung in the breeze. Wide flagstone lanes invited visitors to walk along and gaze at the elaborate Ming Dynasty architecture. She admired the two and three-story buildings of blue bricks and tall pillars that set off snow-white walls. Bright lights illuminated the shopping area where crowds of people lined the streets with artisans' studios of embroidery, porcelain, and a plethora of tea bars. A vendor sold roasted nuts and seeds from his ramshackle stand. Street musicians competed for tokens of gratitude. Anya thought about the war that raged only a short distance away, yet life here seemed almost normal.

A few raindrops fell. Anya opened the umbrella. She pulled the printed note from her pocket and examined it. She had never seen Mac's handwriting before. It was sloppy in that each letter size was inconsistent with the other. Knowing a bit about Mac, it seemed it would be tidy, tight, and trim. Yet, it had his signature. She reread the last few lines of the direction: 'At the first four way crossing, go left. Enter the third teashop on the right.'

A shiver raced from her tailbone to the back of her neck as she paused shy of the teashop. *What if I am heading into a trap?* She heard a dog yip and glanced over her shoulder for a familiar face, but received only stranger's stares. She bit her lip, gripped the umbrella with one hand, and placed the other on the gun in her coat pocket. She took a deep breath and steadied herself. Ready for what awaited her.

TWENTY-SEVEN
Mac

MAC FOUGHT HIS WAY THROUGH THE SERIOUSLY overcrowded streets of the city alone. Ping had told him he had business that needed his attention. Mac contemplated his narrow escape from Yu-seng. Thoughts of his survival for the sake of his family popped up, but he shook them away. He was uncertain of his next move. Exasperated, having seen Anya at Chiang's compound, he scratched his head. *She should have been on her way back to the States. Why is she in Chungking?*

He sat on the remains of a cement stoop in front of a bombed out house. He rested his elbows on his knees and laid his chin on his hands. A chill in the air gave life to his breath as vapors escaped from his mouth. He scanned passers-by.

The streets were teeming with colorful

rickshaws and bicycles. Women in traditional Chinese gowns glided arm-in-arm while men dressed in western attire strode ahead of them. Mac chuckled to himself. He could not imagine Anya walking behind any man.

A leash-less dog sauntered beside a man across the street. *Must be someone with money to care for a pet in these times.* He studied the small man as he neared. His brow furrowed and his eyes blinked as he tried to obtain better focus. He gritted his teeth. Every muscle in his body tightened. *It's Joe.* His conscious refused to shed this man's involvement in his kidnapping in Shanghai.

He was surprised that Joe did not notice him. His attention was elsewhere. Mac rose and crossed the street like a cat after prey. Joe turned the corner. Mac raced to the end of the block and peered around. The distance was too far for him to see whom Joe tailed, but he assumed it was Anya.

A dark silhouette moved in the shadows ahead of him and behind Joe. Mac remained far enough away to insure he was the follower not followed. The shadow crossed under a streetlight, which lit up his appearance. He was slightly taller than Mac and outweighed him by fifty pounds. *Stahl's henchman, Bluto.* Mac chuckled to himself. *I wonder if Segar had him in mind when he created the character in the Popeye comic strip.* He made his way up the street to get closer.

The dog turned, snarled, and then barked but remained by Joe's side. Mac slid between two buildings when Joe stopped in mid-stride. Joe and Bluto caught each other's gaze. Joe nodded as if to say, I know why you are here.

One, two, then three raindrops fell on Mac's head as he slithered between shops and hid among the hordes of people. Mac entered an open-air shopping area that had the appearance of being a village within Chungking. Bluto no longer hid, but walked beside Joe. Even the dog had acquiesced to his presence.

Rain pelted down. Mac lost sight of Joe in a sea of black umbrellas. His heart raced as he searched through the crowd as they jostled him about. *Can't lose him now, too close.*

In his haste, Mac tripped over a peddler's cart. Pots and pans crashed to the ground with a ring that echoed throughout. The proprietor thrashed Mac with a metal ladle. Mac tried to calm the peddler, concerned that the commotion might bring Joe's attention. A grip on Mac's forearm made it difficult for him to flee. He continued to pull away from the peddler when a sudden yelp of a dog caught his attention. "Enough," Mac said. He rammed his thumb into the back of the peddler's hand on his middle tendon. He screamed and released Mac.

Mac pushed his way through the stream of

people and traced his steps back to the yelp. He spotted Joe scoot into a nearby shop. He stretched his neck to see why Joe hid. Down the alleyway, Anya entered a teashop.

TWENTY-EIGHT
Anya

ANYA PREPARED HERSELF. THE SHOP SIGN SAID closed, but she walked in with determination. Intoxicating aromatics filled her nose as she surveyed her surroundings. Hundreds of different shades of teas from brown to black were stacked in clear glass jars from floor to ceiling. The room possessed several wooden tables, empty overstuffed easy chairs, and straight back chairs. A large, benevolent golden Buddha sat in a corner. Ambient light from suspended lanterns cast an afterglow against dark red walls.

She caught sight of a man who pushed aside long bamboo beads used as a curtain. The woody beads clanked together and resonated a hollow tone. Anya sucked in a breath. It was not Mac but Sun Temujin. He wore a dark double-breasted suit that appeared threadbare and his shaggy, coarse black hair needed a trim. He carried his familiar cane in his right hand. The serene calmness that seemed to surround him unnerved her. Their last encounter at the market where he demanded her ring still festered.

"What are you doing here?" Anya said. "Where's Mac?"

He walked over next to her with a sliver of a smile. "Please have a seat, Miss Pavlovitch. We need to talk." Sun sat and leaned his cane against his leg.

"This message is from you?" She extended her arm within inches of Sun's face then crumpled the note in her hand.

"I knew you wouldn't come if it came from me. I am not here to threaten you, but to have a discussion."

Anya believed everything that spewed between his lips were lies. His ultimate goal was to regain the ring. "What about?" She curled her lip.

"Please sit."

Anya pulled the ladder-back chair away from the table and sat, crossed her legs, and folded her arms at her chest. Sun lifted a small, black cast-iron teapot and filled two small white porcelain bowls. "You English like milk and sugar, yes?"

"I'm not English," she snapped. The politeness that seeped from this mercenary made her guts twist.

He lifted his bowl and slurped the tea. "It's

safe," he said. "I've not tampered with the tea. As I said, I am here on a peaceful mission."

"Peace," Anya scoffed. "You don't know the meaning of the word."

Sun's eyes narrowed for a moment then relaxed. He slurped more tea. "You received a ride from a man earlier today."

No response.

"Do you know who this man is?"

No response.

He sat up. His pitch grew loud and guttural. "You know this man."

She glared at him. "I know he controls a drug syndicate in Shanghai and does business with Dai Li."

"Yes, well that's not why you are here." He again slurped his tea.

Her arms tightened against her chest. *If he slurps that tea one more time, I swear, I will throw it in his face.*

"You had mentioned to Yu-seng that Li's life was in danger. He wants to know who's behind this threat. I have my suspicions, but want to hear it from you."

Anya's body stiffened. If she were to disclose Mac's involvement, she would not only be trying to outmaneuver Stahl, but Sun and Yu-seng. Her head pounded. *I could really use the cavalry.* "What makes you believe I would work with you?"

Sun raised his eyebrows, cocked his head and smirked, "I know the location of Commander Benson."

Anya gulped. *Could he possibly have Mac captive, again? Did he try to beat Mac's mission out of him but he wouldn't talk and now he wants me to spill the beans?*

"If you give me the information I seek," he leaned forward, "I will tell you where you can find him."

"What assurance do I have that you will tell me the truth? You have not been forthcoming in the past."

His lifeless black eyes met hers. "We no longer have any interest in this man."

She battled confusion. *Did he kill Mac? Does he believe I'm the assassin?* She swallowed hard. *Where is Superman when you need him?*

Sun refreshed his tea and then slurped it.

Anya jumped up ready to slap the bowl out of his hands when Joe bounded through the front door. Her heart raced. Droplets of sweat formed on her palms. Her eyes shifted from Joe to Bluto. *Has Joe betrayed me to Sun and Stahl? Even the dog seems to side against me.* She wiped her hands on her pants legs.

Surrounded, a steadfast need to escape seized her, but Bluto's muscular physique blocked the front entrance. Sun sat between her and the back exit. If she toppled Sun from his seat, it would block Joe's path and allow her to make a break for it. The sudden hollow sound from the beads that wavered caught her attention. She went to make her move…

Joe raised his hands, palms up. "Anya, this isn't how it looks." He caught his breath. "You seemed upset so I followed you. Hei-Hei and I are here to protect you." He sneered at Sun.

Sun placed his tea on the table and chuckled. "It's Mr. Henderson's little friend."

"Devil." Joe spat on the floor. "I know you killed him."

Sun rocked back in his chair. "I see you have acquired a new friend."

Bluto grunted and puffed out his chest. Joe advanced towards Sun. Hei-Hei snarled at his side.

Sun sprang from his seat. His cane crashed to the ground. He pulled a Tokarev pistol from inside his vest and pointed it at the dog. "I'd think twice before making your next move, sonny boy."

Joe motioned the dog to remain by his side. Anya knew if she went for her Beretta, Sun would gun down Joe. Bluto advanced when Anya yelled out. "Hold it. Joe, you and Bluto need to leave. Sun and I are only having a conversation." Although she feared for her own life, she did not want Joe in the middle.

"That's right, boy," Sun said. "The adults are having a discussion."

Anya placed her hands together as if to pray and motioned for Joe to exit.

"All right, gramps, but if any harm comes to her you'll answer to me." Joe said to Anya, "We'll wait for you outside."

Joe and Bluto turned to exit when Hei-Hei lifted his nose and sniffed the air. The dog growled then positioned himself between Joe and the back entrance. All eyes focused on the bamboo beads. The back door creaked and a gust of air wafted through. The dog took off before Joe could control him. Anya seized the opportunity and ran out the front.

TWENTY-NINE
Mac

MAC DARTED OUT THE BACK DOOR OF THE teashop when he heard the dog bark. A voice yelled out, "Check the back." The dog was close on his tail when he slammed the door on its snout. He heard the dog yelp as he took off down the alley into a crowd. He half-turned several times to see if anyone had followed.

How was Sun not dead? He'd no pulse with a bullet in his gut. Man, that bastard has more lives than a cat.

Mac scrunched down and blended among the mass of umbrellas as raindrops pelted him. He flipped his coat collar up around his neck and hailed a rickshaw.

He wiped the water off his face and thought about Anya's involvement. He slammed his fist into the palm of his other hand. *Why would she rat on me?*

He had the rickshaw runner stop a block from the entry to his rented flat. A shadow cased the place. *Damn, Stahl no doubt.* He motioned for the runner to turn around.

Mac had been to Ping's place once. Fortunately, he had a good sense of direction. The light of the sunrise lit the sky with yellow and orange streaks. He trotted down the cement steps beside a bombed-out English brownstone into the basement of a hole in the ground. He moved the unhinged plywood board that provided a door. Puddles of water saturated the cement floor, and the smell of sour rot filled the air. Mac sidestepped his way towards a dim light at the end of the hall.

Ping did not look up when Mac entered the room. He continued to rummage through a stack of papers with a cigarette adhered to his lips. When he did notice him, Ping scrunched up a piece of paper and placed it in his pocket.

"What you do here?" Smoke escaped from Ping's mouth as he spoke.

"The cops are casing my joint."

Ping wrinkled his brow. "Huh?"

"I need to sort some things out." Mac flopped lengthwise on a dilapidated davenport and flung his legs over the edge. He used his trench coat as a blanket then folded his arm over his eyes. "I need to get a few winks. Wake me in a couple of hours."

MAC WOKE TO THE SOUND of a voice speaking in Chinese. He scanned the room and tried to conjure up his location. Paint flakes the color of mud were scattered about the floor. Broken pipes hung from the ceiling. An open door led to a washroom. The chilly room accommodated two chairs, desk and the daveno where he lay.

Ping ended his conversation and returned the phone receiver to its cradle.

"Who was that?" Mac said.

"My brother." Ping lowered his eyes.

Mac scratched his head, sat up, stretched and yawned. "What time is it?"

"Noon."

Mac jumped to his feet. "You should have woken me earlier."

Ping lifted his head and faced Mac. "I try, but you fling arm at me and say get lost."

Mac headed to the washroom and splashed cold water on his stubble. He used his index finger to brush his teeth then ran his wet hands through his shaggy hair.

He took a hard look at himself in the mirror. His cheekbones were more pronounced, and he had taken in his belt an extra notch. "Buddy, you could use a cut, a shave and a hot meal." He popped his head out from the washroom. "I need your help today."

Ping yanked open a desk drawer and rummaged through it.

"What the hell are you looking for?"

Ping slammed the drawer shut with one hand behind his back. "Nothing."

Mac squinted at him with a furrowed brow but decided not to pursue it. His attention was on more matters of importance. He returned to the bathroom. "Do you remember that woman we saw the other day?"

Ping replied, "Ya."

"I need to find her." Mac tucked his shirt into his trousers, stepped out from the bathroom, grabbed his trench coat, and the two set out.

He decided to stake out the area where he first encountered Joe. He assumed they must be staying in the area. Ping sat on the cement stoop while Mac hid in the shadows between two buildings. He hoped to catch Anya returning after being out all day.

They had waited nearly four hours when Mac spotted Anya. Joe and the dog were not in sight. He motioned for Ping to stay put. Mac crossed the street, snuck up to her, grabbed her upper arm, and pulled her around the corner. He pushed her up against the brick building and shielded her from passersby as though the two were in a lovers embrace.

"Explain yourself."

Anya's eyes widened and a smile crossed her face. "Thank God, you're still alive."

"Of course I am. Why wouldn't I be?"

"Sun isn't dead."

"I know. I saw him at the teashop."

"So, you're the one the dog was after. Your life is at risk. People…" Anya fought to free his grasp. "…are trying to kill you."

"You mean Stahl and his goon. I wish them luck."

"This is not a joke. You're to return home either standing up or in a pine box."

"I have a job to do and I plan to complete it." He squeezed her arm. When she winced, he loosened his hold.

"You muttonhead. Your mission has been cancelled. C A N C E L L E D. That's what everyone has been trying to get through that thick skull of yours."

"Those were Atwater's orders," Mac said. "I take my orders from Donovan."

"OWI, OSS, NI. It's an alphabet party and they are all in it together."

"What were you doing meeting with Sun? You're now in cahoots with him too?"

"You've got it all wrong. I thought you wrote me a note to meet you. Then Sun showed up, to my surprise, and said he knew where I could find you."

Mac felt a slap on his shoulder and swung around. Ping stood in front of him breathless. His arm stretched out as he pointed down the street. Lumbering towards them at a fast pace was Bluto.

For all those muscles, Bluto proved to be slow on his feet. However, Bluto was the type that once in his clutches, you had no choice but to yield, and Mac had no intention of surrendering.

"Your henchman, Madame?" Mac released his grip and took off with Ping close behind.

Anya rubbed her arm and yelled out, "I'm not the enemy."

MAC AND PING HAD MANAGED to out maneuver Bluto. They arrived back at his place before dark. Mac sank into the dank odorous cushions of the daveno and thought about his plight. *What if the mission's been scrapped?* He thought about what that would mean—going back home to his wife and daughter. *I could be ready to go home. I'm sick of this cat and mouse game.* Mac sat up and rested his chin on his fist. *If what she said is true, then Anya could be in danger from Sun.*

No matter what she had done or whom she was working with, she needed his help. The challenge would be to help her and avoid getting gunned down in the process.

THIRTY

Anya

ANYA RUBBED AWAY THE STING FROM MAC'S constricted grip on her arm as she watched him run down the road. Along his path, he shoved pedestrians aside. A few fell to the ground screaming and cursing.

A boy followed Mac. She was glad he had befriended someone. Someone he could trust to help him out of scrapes. But she wondered about the scar on his face. *Was he friend or foe?*

A whiff of pungent sweat swept past her as Bluto ran by. She shook her head and muttered. "You fool. You'll never catch him on foot." She continued to watch the folly. *If only Mac had listened to my earlier plea to give up this worthless mission, the whole thing would be over, and we would be on our way back to the States.* "God, what a pig-headed man."

Anya spun around on her heels and gasped. Her skin turned clammy, and her heart thumped. She found herself alone, face-to-face with Sun. He sported a black fedora and cape and slapped his cane against his palm. A sweet sickening odor spewed off him. "What the hell are you doing here?" She spoke with a clenched jaw that made her sound like Katherine Hepburn.

Sun gave her a sideways sliver-thin smile. "We meet again." A familiar shiny black sedan drove up and screeched to a stop alongside the curb. She recognized the driver and the car. It was the Rolls-Royce that had offered her and Joe a ride at Chiang's compound. Her survival instincts kicked in. She went to flee when Sun grabbed her upper arm. The former sting returned. She struggled to free his grip, and agonized over having left her gun in the room.

She heard tapping from above and looked up. Joe peered down from their rented room. She locked her knees to try to prevent Sun from pushing her into the sedan. Cold metal touched her cheek, and she froze. The end of Sun's cane held a six-inch blade. The same knife he had used to kill her parents.

She remembered how Sun had gloated when he told her about the 1920 incident in Shanghai. The combination of fear and rage consumed her thoughts. She wished she had Joe's combative skills to thwart this villain.

"Get in," he said.

The fury in his crazy eyes frightened her more than at any other encounter. "What… do…you want?" She tried to catch her breath.

"Just get in." The point of the blade rested against her collarbone.

A slight tremble moved up her spine as she entered the back of the car. She caught her right foot on the running board and fell into the backseat. The chauffeur faced her with a sinister grin. She scurried to right herself. Mac had run off and Joe was upstairs, too far to help. Her mind reeled. *Stay calm. Stay focused. Stay alive.*

The apartment front door flung open with an abrupt crash against the side of the building. Joe and Hei-Hei ran out. Sun jumped in, slammed the car door shut, and ordered the driver to step on it. Anya turned to look out the back window. She heard Hei-Hei bark as he chased after the car. Joe's face said it all. She was in deep trouble.

Anya mouthed to Joe, "Find Mac."

Joe nodded as his image grew smaller and smaller until it was out of sight. She fell back in her seat. All hope to survive rested on Joe.

The sedan raced through the rutted streets of Chungking. She looked for a way to signal to Chinese soldiers along the route, but they passed by too quickly for her to communicate. The driver took a corner too sharp and tossed her into Sun. Sun momentarily lost his grip on his cane. Anya went for the door handle. She figured even at the speed they were going, she could roll onto the ground with a minimal of cuts and abrasions. The handle was gone. Escape seemed hopeless.

Anya dug deep inside herself to find something to cling to that would calm her nerves. She recalled Mac's words, "Never show your emotions. It can save your life."

She wiped her moist palms on her pants legs and steadied her voice. "Why does Du Yu-seng want to see me?"

Sun let out a guttural laugh.

"Did I say something funny?"

"This has nothing to do with Yu-Seng or Li," he hissed.

"Then what is this about?"

"Revenge, my dear. This is about revenge."

"Revenge?" Her face reddened.

"You and your friend left me for dead. I want to do the same for you."

"If you're going to kill me, then…do it and be done with it."

"First, my ring." He held his hand out.

"It's my ring. I don't have it on me. It's back in my room," she lied. Anya knew enough not to touch or look at her breast and give away its true location.

"I will send someone to retrieve it." He twirled his cane. "In the encounter, he may injure your friend."

"He knows nothing. You don't need to hurt him."

"Then you will write a note and have him bring it. Until then, we wait for the one who is yet to arrive." Sun rested his head on the back seat and laughed.

THIRTY-ONE
Mac

AN ABRUPT KNOCK AT THE DOOR CAUSED MAC and Ping to freeze. Mac thought he had eluded Bluto, but now questioned whether he had discovered their location and brought reinforcements. He grabbed his Remington from his inside coat pocket.

Mac whispered, "Are you expecting someone?"

"No." Ping shook his head. "No one."

Mac braced himself inside the door with weapon in hand. Ping slowly opened it.

The voice on the other side of the door said, "I need to speak to Mister Mac."

The hairs on Mac's neck bristled. He knew in an instant, it was Joe's voice. He holstered his gun. This was personal. Mac flew around the door and wrapped his fingers around Joe's neck.

Hei-Hei bared his teeth and snarled. Joe gave the dog a hand signal to stand down. "Ma…ac…l…le…t go," Joe choked out. He tried to pull Mac's hands away from his neck. "Ahh…Ahh…nya."

Mac loosened his grip. "What about her?"

"Sun has Anya."

"She is working with him now," Mac said.

"You have it all wrong. She has been trying to track you down to save you from certain death."

Mac released his grip. Joe collapsed to the ground. Hei-Hei licked Joe's face.

"How the hell did you find me?" Mac said.

Joe staggered to his feet and rubbed his neck. "It wasn't easy." He caught his breath. "I had some assistance."

"Stahl?" Mac said.

"No. A local resistance group we met through a contact of mine in Shinjing."

Mac noticed Ping's body stiffen and his eyes shifted to the floor. "Do you know these people?" Ping shook his head, avoiding Mac's gaze.

"Look," Joe said. "I know you're still upset about Shanghai. I'm sorry, but you don't understand about family loyalty. It is very important in my culture. Without family what is there?"

The faces of Mac's wife and daughter flashed in his mind. He thought about how quick he had rushed to take the assignment. How quick he had abandoned them with little regard. How quick he had considered only himself. He felt corroded by regret.

"I am on yours and Anya's side," Joe said. "I came to Chungking with her to locate you and protect her from Sun. Unfortunately, you don't believe in her loyalty, and Sun is too cunning and slick." He continued to massage his throat. "Anya asked me to find you. She said, 'if we ever get into trouble, Mac will help.' So…will you?"

Mac gave Joe a hard look. He thought about how Anya had been upfront with him, and how he had come to rely on her in the past. *She deserves my allegiance.* It took him a few seconds to relent and relax his muscles. "Have a seat."

Joe sniffed the air, looked about the studio, crinkled his nose and said, "Thanks, I'll stand."

Mac stepped over to the desk, picked up the phone and dialed the operator. "Connect me to the American Embassy. Yes. Chungking. I don't know the bloody address. I don't want to write a letter, I just want to make a bloody phone call." Mac raked his fingers through his hair and paced alongside the desk.

He stopped in mid-stride. "Yes, American Embassy? Connect me with Luther Stahl." Mac paused and listened.

"I don't care if he's got the goddamn Pope in his office. Tell him it's a matter of someone's life." Mac placed the mouthpiece up against his chest. "Can you believe these people?"

He returned the receiver to his ear. "Stahl, Benson here. I need your assistance. A friend has been kidnapped. Yes…yes…but…he is a very dangerous man."

Mac rolled his eyes at Joe. "Let it go. I'm not coming in. No, I'm not. I said no."

Mac hung his head and sighed. "I've made the decision to abort that mission. I've got a new assignment.

"Can you help or not? Yes. I know. But she is a U.S. citizen for Christ's sake." Mac slammed the phone in its cradle.

"They say their hands are tied and are unable to get involved with local matters. What a pack of hypocrites. I have a good mind to…"

"Never mind, Mac," Joe said. "We can obtain backing elsewhere."

MAC AND JOE STOOD at the doorstep of Guo's place. Ping had told Mac he would recruit a few others and meet him back at the studio. Ping's earlier reaction to Joe's reference to Shinjing weighed on Mac, but he decided to speak with Ping about it later.

"Let's hope these guys will assist us," Mac said

as Joe knocked on the door. A loose hinge caused a squeak as it opened. A barefoot boy with sunken black eyes stared up at them.

"Guo," Joe said.

The boy turned and trotted down the hall leaving the door partially opened. Mac poked his head in and scanned inside. The room housed several chairs and a ratty rug. There were no usual accessories similar to the ones found in fashionable homes. Sheets hung loosely on the windows. A musty smell like a wet dog lingered. It was a far cry from his monochromatic modern home back in the States.

A gaunt figure of a man wearing a soiled white tunic and pants strode at them like a mechanical doll. Joe pushed his way ahead of Mac and spoke to him in Mandarin. "Guo, my dear friend. It's good to see you again."

Guo returned the bow then crinkled his brow at Mac.

"This is a compatriot of Anya's," Joe said. "He is the one I asked you to help me locate."

Guo put his hands together, placed them at his forehead, and bowed. He straightened up and addressed Joe.

Joe translated. "He says you are welcome in his home. Anya is in great favor with him."

Mac smiled. "She tends to grow on you."

Joe spoke to Guo, who nodded several times and grunted with wild arm gestures. Several members of Guo's gang entered the room. They circled around Mac as though they were inspecting a priceless object.

Joe faced Mac. "I have explained that we need him and his gang to locate Anya. He has agreed and wants to know how they can assist."

"Well…" Mac scratched his head. "First we need to find out where this villain has her held hostage."

"That might not be so easy," Joe said.

"Guo found me, so I'm certain they can do the same for Anya." He pointed to Guo. "Translate."

Joe accommodated his request

Guo clapped his hands and his followers huddled around him then took off to the street like a pack on the hunt.

"They will return with the information," Joe said. "In the meantime, I must return to the flat and retrieve Anya's gun. We can always use another weapon."

JOE AND MAC ARRIVED at Joe's place and discovered a note on the floor. Mac picked it up and read it.

"It's probably a bill from the landlady," Joe said.

"It's from Anya. She wants you to bring her ring." He hesitated. "I thought she always kept that close to her heart." He pointed to his chest.

"It's pinned to her undergarment." Joe's face blushed. "I don't understand. Is it some kind of a code?"

"I think what she is trying to tell us where she is being held. The note has the name of a hotel, but no address."

"Maybe Guo knows the place," Joe said.

Mac rubbed his chin. "Seems too easy." He paced. "Out in the open. In a hotel. Not a secluded empty warehouse. Something's wrong." He stopped and turned to Joe. "He wants an exchange."

"What do you mean?" Joe said.

"I know this man like my own birthmark. He wants me."

"Why?"

"The oldest reason in the world, revenge."

THIRTY-TWO
Mac

PING HAD NOT RETURNED TO HIS FLAT AS planned. Mac believed he had always been reliable. He wondered what would have caused him to falter now. Earlier, Ping had rummaged through his desk. Mac got curious and walked over. He pulled out a drawer. Deep in the back, he found a box of .45 ammo…no gun. Time being precious, he could not ponder on it nor look for him.

MAC AND JOE FOLLOWED Guo and his gang to the location of the hotel stated on Anya's note. The five-story square building's front façade held colorful tiles embedded in a mosaic pattern. Tall arched windows gave the appearance of a middle-eastern mosque. A Nationalist flag flew overhead. The hotel, partially dug into the hillside, had suffered little damage from the massive air raids of the past.

GUO AND HIS MEN staged themselves in different parts of the hotel. A couple of guys with the dog were stationed outside in the event Sun attempted to flee. Mac and Joe entered through the kitchen. The staff did not seem to notice nor care and without missing a beat, continued to prepare the days meal.

The scuttlebutt around the hotel was that a western woman and an eastern man were seen together on the third level. Mac and Joe used the staff elevator to reach the floor where they believed Anya was held hostage. They stepped off the elevator into a long, empty hallway. The carpet looked in need of cleaning and the walls a good scrub. They crept and listened at each door for a familiar voice.

"Anything?" Mac said.

Joe shrugged. "A flushed toilet."

They turned the corner and encountered a maid several yards away in the middle of the hallway. She grabbed a few towels from her cart and entered a guest's room.

"Let's circle back the other way to avoid being seen by her."

"Wait," Joe said. He then walked down the hall to meet the maid.

"Damn it, get back here," Mac said in a sotto

voice. *God, he knows nothing about stealth.*

Mac watched from around the corner as Joe spoke to the maid. She pointed in Mac's direction. Mac jerked his head back to hide. He grabbed Joe by the collar as he came around the corner. "What the hell? Are you trying to foul things up?"

"I'm getting fed up with your hands on me." Joe straightened his tunic after Mac released his grip. "These people don't care about anything but their own lives. If someone were dying they would vacuum around them."

"What did she say?"

"They're in room 320."

"Did you get a description?"

Joe cocked his head and gave Mac a blank stare.

"Right, they just vacuum. Let's check it out."

They reached room 320. Mac believed he heard voices. He motioned to Joe to stop and wait. He tiptoed up to the door and placed his ear against it. Mac waived Joe over and whispered, "Knock and say in a high-pitched voice, 'maid service.'"

Joe complied. The voices on the other side of the door went silent. Joe repeated, "Maid service."

A man's voice replied, "We don't need anything. Go away."

Joe looked up at Mac and twisted his lips.

Mac said, "Tell him you have a message to deliver."

Joe complied again.

Mac heard the latch come off, and the door opened. He kicked it inward and heard the thud of a body hit the ground. He took two steps inside and sucked in a breath. His eyes narrowed and his face reddened with anger. Sprawled on the floor holding a bleeding nose lay Ping.

Ping struggled to his feet. Mac pushed him back down and held him with his foot. "Et tu Brutus? Now know how Julius Caesar felt."

Ping snarled up at him.

"Where's Sun?" Mac said.

Anya stood beside a chair. "Don't know."

Mac pressed on Ping's throat. "Where is he?"

Ping choked out, "Lobby."

Mac returned his attention to Anya. He noticed a small table had a service of tea and cakes. "You seem relaxed given the circumstance."

"His idea of a last meal." She tilted her head to the table. "He seems to think I'm English."

Joe piped in, "Shouldn't we be thinking about getting out of here?"

"Just a minute," Mac said. He lifted Ping off the ground and smashed his fist square on his jaw. Ping's head flung back and he fell unconscious. "Okay, now we can go."

The three stepped out into the hallway as Sun closed the metal gate to the elevator. Mac drew his

Remington and fired a shot. Sun returned to the elevator, but the lift had been called for and it headed up. He ran in the opposite direction. Mac fired again. The bullet ricocheted off the edge of the wall as Sun dashed around the corner. The three chased after him. They turned the corner to find the hallway deserted.

"Did he dart into one of the rooms?" Anya said.

Mac took a step and then stopped. He faced a square metal flap in the wall. "He's escaped through the laundry shoot." Mac ran to the stairs exit sign and raced down, skipping steps.

Anya and Joe tried to keep up, but Mac was almost to the first floor while they were still on the third. Anya lost her footing. She missed the last few steps and bounced on her derriere to the next floor landing. She moaned and grabbed her ankle.

"Are you all right?" Joe said.

She winced and rubbed her ankle

Joe helped Anya up as she applied pressure and attempted to walk. "I'm okay, just twisted it a bit, but I can continue."

They no longer heard Mac as the two descended to the basement, albeit a bit slower this time. But they did hear the screech of the metal elevator gate being pulled and then slammed shut.

MAC INCHED HIS WAY into a humid room with a rank odor. A gray cement washbasin stood against one wall. Overhead, sunlight streamed in from the small half opened window. In another area, linen hung to dry on rope lines.

A sudden loud crash echoed behind him. It triggered a flinch. He whipped around. A bundle of white sheets lay on the ground. A second, then third bundle dropped from the ceiling. He took a deep breath and exhaled.

A noise alerted his attention and he headed in the direction. His arm, gun in hand, extended as he crossed through an entryway. A wallop followed by a sharp pain to his wrist caused him to drop the gun. He recognized the cane, but before he could react, the muzzle of a gun jammed hard against his back.

THIRTY-THREE
Mac

MAC DID NOT NEED TO TURN AROUND TO SEE WHO had a gun on his back. Ping pushed him into the room with the end of the barrel.

"Stick up," Ping said.

"It's, stick 'em up, you idiot." Mac swaggered in with raised arms. It was not the first time Sun held an advantage on him.

"Nice .45," he said to Ping. His voice betrayed no stress just a bit of sarcasm.

Ping picked up Mac's Remington off the floor and placed it beside Sun.

"Where are the rest of your club members?" Sun twirled his cane.

Mac's lips remained tight.

Ping spoke to Sun in Mandarin. "I heard them clomping down the stairwell. They should be here momentarily." He directed a sneer at Mac.

Mac refused to acknowledge Ping's slight and looked at Sun. "Mind if I put my hands down?"

Sun sat on a folding table next to a stack of white towels. His legs dangled and swung in a casual manner. He nodded.

Ping stood rigid with the muzzle of a gun pointed at Mac's temple. Mac figured he could easily get the gun away from the shifty dog. However, Sun's deceptive cane and a gun at his side presented a challenge.

The sudden click-clack from heels down the hallway interrupted his thoughts. All heads turned to face the opened door.

ANYA AND JOE ALMOST walked past the doorway. They stopped in mid-stride. A flood of heat coursed through her body when she saw the gun directed at Mac. Words failed her.

"Glad you could join us," Sun said. He hopped off the table and twirled his cane. "Seems like old times—the three of us."

Anya swallowed hard. Her mind flashed back to the knife she had thrust into his thigh. Mac had shot him in the gut and the two had left him for dead. How he had managed to survived escaped her, but she knew his revenge ensued certainty.

Her eyes shifted from Mac to Ping then darted back to Mac. "I thought," she pointed to Ping, "he was on your side."

Mac shrugged. "Not a very good judge of character."

Joe flushed red with shame at how he had deceived Mac and Anya in Shanghai.

Ping puffed up his chest. "I fool you good. All time I away, I meet my master."

Mac glared at him. He recalled how suspicious it seemed when they first met. Ping happened to be at just the right place and time. He remembered Ping had disappeared in search of food at Chiang's compound and then had to attend to business. "I thought I'd smelled the stench of betrayal."

Anya studied Ping's facial scar then noticed a familiar tattoo on his forearm. It was the same freedom mark worn by the Shinjing resistance. She remembered that one of their own had sided with the enemy. Zang had said they slashed him to mark him as a traitor, but he eluded capture. "You're from Shinjing," she burst out. "You betrayed your own people to the Japanese."

Ping slouched and hung his head like a whipped puppy. Sun moved to Ping's side and patted his back. "He has been most valuable to me. I found him on the streets starving and gave him something to eat." Sun moved his hand to Ping's head and petted him. "You see, if you feed a hungry dog, he will follow you anywhere."

Anya would not relent. "But why?"

Ping regained his backbone. "I need better life."

Sun tilted his head back and laughed. "Greed. It's the way of the world."

"Not everyone is like both of you." Anya's voice reached a high pitch. "My father, an honorable man, cherished his country and the people until those damn Bolsheviks came into power."

"Those people paid me a lot of money for your father's life."

Anya balled her hand into a fist and lunged at Sun. Mac grabbed her by the arm. "He's not worth your anger." He whispered into her ear. "Don't forget that cane."

Sun pulled the cap off his cane exposing the six-inch blade.

Mac placed himself in front of Anya and addressed Sun. "How did you know I'd be in Chungking?"

"There are many eyes in China. It is not difficult to track a tall American out of uniform. Plus, I knew you would find me." Sun tilted his head at Anya.

"You can go back to Dai Li and assure him the hunt is over," Mac said.

Sun snorted. "I am no longer concerned about Li's wellbeing."

"Then what do you want?"

"You and that woman." Sun touched his belly.

"You left me to die."

Anya stepped beside Mac and spoke to Sun. "You killed my parents, you filthy bugger. I would have finished you off had I known you were still alive."

Sun lunged forward in an attempt to stab Anya. He exposed the cane's handle close to Mac. Mac seized the cane. They both wrestled for control. Joe thrust his leg and kicked the gun out of Ping's hand. It slid across the floor. The two jumped for it. Ping's hand reached for the barrel, but the force of his outstretched fingers pushed the gun towards Joe, who grabbed it.

Mac gained possession of the cane and went for Sun. Sun spun around to the table where Mac's gun lay. He picked it up, turned, and fired.

The room fell silent and the fighting ceased. Mac's right upper arm spewed blood. Sun's trigger finger was ready to pull back and fire again.

"Wait," she shouted.

Sun and Mac swung around and faced Anya.

"Let's make a deal."

Sun's coal black eyes narrowed. "What kind of a deal?"

"I have something you want."

"Such as?"

"A red Asscher ring." She dug under her blouse, unpinned the ring from her brassiere, and showed it to Sun. The center red diamond surrounded by sapphires and white diamonds cast a brilliant sparkle.

Sun's eyes fixated on the object and he wet his lips. "So, you had it all the time. You little she-devil. I should have searched you myself."

"No, Anya," Mac said. Blood seeped between his fingers as he tried to stop the bleeding.

"It's okay, Mac. Your life has more value than my ring."

"He has my gun. Once you give him your ring he will shoot us."

"No he won't," Joe said. "I have a gun on Ping."

Mac turned to Joe. "He doesn't give a plugged nickel for that man's life. He'd just as soon shoot him too."

"He's right, sonny boy," Sun said.

Joe stepped behind and to the right of Ping and pointed the gun at Sun. "Then I'll shoot you instead."

Mac grinned at Sun. "Checkmate."

THIRTY-FOUR
Anya and Mac

SUN WAVED HIS GUN FIRST AT MAC THEN AT Anya. "If either of you move, it'll be fatal." Vapors escaped from his nose and mouth in the cold damp laundry room of the hotel basement. A noxious odor infused the atmosphere. Tension was high. Everyone remained primed.

Mac continued to apply pressure to his wound. The steeliness in Sun's tone required cautious tact. He bumped into Anya to snap her out of any thoughts of retaliation.

Joe countered Sun's threat. "If you shoot, I'll take you down."

Sun returned a sideways smile.

Mac hoped Sun's response was bravado rather than a visceral reaction to Joe's slight tremble.

"Let's everyone remain calm." Anya had felt

Mac's elbow on her back and remained calm. "We can work this out so everyone comes out ahead."

Mac said out of the corner of his mouth, "he needs to make peace with his God."

"Mac…" Anya sighed. "You're not helping." She advanced, but made sure Joe still had a clear shot. "Keep in mind that Joe is an excellent marksman," she lied. "We don't need any more bloodshed." She looked at Mac, and then continued. "I'm going to hand over my ring."

"Don't, Anya." Mac collapsed to the floor beside his coagulated blood.

Anya stretched out her arm to Sun. A nervous quiver ran down its length. The ring lay nestled in her damp palm. Sun reached forward and snatched the ring. The weightlessness in her hand gave way to nausea. Bile filled her mouth.

A sinister grin crossed Sun's face as he slowly backed up toward the door. Ping approached Sun.

"You stay," Sun said. "I don't need you anymore."

Anya thought she heard Ping whimper.

"I told you he'd just as soon kill ya," Mac muttered.

The instant Sun vanished, Anya ordered Ping to remove his tunic. Joe nudged Ping with the barrel of the Remington and he complied. Anya tore it in two strips and wrapped one tight around Mac's upper arm above the wound to stem the bleeding. She handed him the other piece to wipe his bloodstained hand.

"Joe, go find Guo and hunt down Sun."

"What about this guy?" He pointed to Ping.

Anya continued to dress Mac's wound. "You can shoot him for all I care."

Ping cried out.

"What shall we do with him, Mac?" she said.

Mac grinned. "Feed him to hungry sharks." His smile lingered only a moment. "Let him go. He's not worth our time."

"Get out," Anya yelled. Ping took off without hesitation.

Anya placed Mac's uninjured arm around her shoulder.

"I can manage by myself," he said.

"You've lost a lot of blood." She prodded him to move and assisted him to the elevator. "Seems you're always getting hurt, and I'm always nursing you back to health."

"You know, you need to let me be the hero once in a while."

Anya laughed. "I'll work on it." They entered the elevator and she pressed the number one button.

Mac's voice took on a grave tone. "Sorry about the ring."

"I'll get it back."

They rode the elevator up and arrived at the front lobby. Joe stood before them breathless. "They….tried….to capture Sun, but he got away."

Anya slid the metal gate aside and they stepped out onto a cream-colored marble floor. She guided Mac to a chair and sat him down.

Joe continued, "Apparently, there's a secret corridor used to evacuate guests during bombing raids. Some of Guo's men have taken Hei-Hei and are trying to track Sun. I'm going after them."

Anya watched Joe run to the basement steps.

"You want to go, don't you?" Mac said.

"Yes, but you need me."

"I'll be okay. Go on," he urged her.

Anya believed there were enough people around to see that he received medical attention. She waived over a hotel manager then squeezed Mac's forearm and left in pursuit.

ANYA'S ANKLE WAS STILL TENDER, but she powered through the pain and rushed down the basement steps after Joe. His footsteps echoed up the staircase, but he was too far ahead for her to see him. At the bottom, she spotted him at the end of the hallway. Anya hastened her pace. She crossed through a doorway that led to the escape tunnel. Her feet sloshed through water that had settled on the floor. Anya had caught up with Joe by the time she reached the end of the passageway.

A door led to an outside stairwell. They climbed to the top and stepped out onto a grassy field. A splash of colored spring wild flowers had began to sprout along the hillside. The smell, like fresh cut grass from a recent rain, permeated the air.

"I hear Hei-Hei's bark," Joe said. "This way."

Anya had no time to catch her breath before they were off again. Adrenaline was the only thing that kept her moving. They sprinted along a rutted muddy path. The dog's bark grew increasingly louder as they made their way down a small ravine. At one point, she slipped on a wet patch but caught her balance. A strong stench filled her nostrils as they neared a creek. Guo and his men stood and waited. Hei-Hei ran to greet Joe.

"Why…," Anya inhaled deeply, "have you stopped?"

"Sun must have waded through the sewage run-off." Guo pointed to the stream. "We tracked him for several yards, but the dog lost his scent."

Joe knelt and massaged Hei-Hei's ears. "It's okay. You did good."

"He'll want to get out of China." Anya pushed a lock of hair away from her face. "He'll either make his way to India or south to Indochina. We should monitor the docks by the river."

"I'll have my men scout around and get back to

you. Hopefully we can find him in short order," Guo said.

A LOUD BOAT HORN BLASTED. Crewmembers hollered at perspective passengers to hurry. People scurried along the wooden pier carrying large bundles; a few toted toddlers. They boarded junks, sampans, or ships, all destined for other parts along the Yangtze. Diesel fuel permeated every molecule in the air and seeped into the river. Chinese navy cruised the river while the infantry monitored the shoreline. To the untrained eye, chaos reigned.

Anya arrived at the river's edge where Guo and his men had boarded a seventy-foot wooden junk with its single tattered sail hoisted. The rig itself looked sturdy although, it had seen better days.

"Bad news," Guo said. "Sun's not on this junk. We think he managed to sneak aboard another ship, headed up-river, maybe enroute to India. I've secured passage. The captain is willing to take us upstream."

"I'd like you to take Joe. I'll catch up with you in a few days."

Joe's bottom lip began to quiver.

Anya placed her hand on his arm. "I need you to do this for me."

ANYA STOOD ON THE DOCK, several steps from the plank where Joe was to board. She twisted her finger and sighed. "There's so much I want to say, but fragmented words spin round in my brain, and I can't put a proper goodbye together."

"I know." Joe took her hand. "I'll miss you too."

Anya wrapped her arms around Joe and squeezed tight. "I will always consider you a part of my family—my Chinese brother." She released her embrace. "I wish I could go with you, but I'm afraid Stahl might try to send Mac home before he is stable enough to travel."

"It has been my pleasure to assist you, Miss Anya." Joe bowed. "Don't worry. We will find Sun and return your ring.

"Mac and I couldn't have succeeded without your help." She knelt and wrapped her arms around the dog's neck. "You too, you old hound dog." She returned to her feet.

Joe climbed aboard the ship. Hei-Hei jumped in and panted with excitement. "Oh, might want to let Mac know that Guo's men have Ping." Joe winked and waived. "I'll be in touch."

Anya watched the junk traverse the crowded harbor. She wanted to shout, "Wait for me." But he was out of earshot before the words came to her throat. A familiar emptiness consumed her. Once again, she was alone.

THIRTY-FIVE
Anya and Mac

THE CLOUDS HAD VANISHED FOR THE FIRST TIME in days. Anya and Mac drenched themselves in the warmth of the sunlight outside the air terminal. The ramshackle wooden building looked as though a strong wind could topple it. Dirt-covered windows flung open and several unarmed Chinese soldiers hung halfway out. In the distance, a large transport plane was parked on the airstrip. It resembled a gray whale. A squadron of solid green P-40 Tomahawks awaited their next fight.

"What's he doing here?" Anya referred to Stahl, who stood in the doorway.

"Orders. He has to make sure I board the plane."

The two stood in silence for several minutes. Neither made eye contact with the other. A flock of geese honked as they flew overhead. "It's rare to see them in these parts. It's a good omen," Anya said.

Awkward silence lingered.

"I'll miss China," Mac said. He kicked at the dirt. "You know, I never wanted you on this mission. I believed you were assigned to watch over me. I let that get in the way." He paused and looked her straight in the eye. "You're okay in my book." He turned his head away. "I wanted you to know that."

Anya's face flushed. "It's time for you to return to your wife and daughter who are waiting for you back home."

"What about you?"

"Guo thinks they found the boat Sun escaped on. I should have my ring back in a few days."

"How do you feel about that?"

"What do you mean?"

"Sun, being alive."

She shrugged. "All I care about is the retrieval of my ring."

"What if they can't find him and you don't get it back?"

"I'll hunt him down until its back in my possession." Her face flushed red. She looked over at the plane. "They're calling you to board."

Mac shook her hand and held on to it longer than protocol dictated. "See ya round sister." He turned and ambled to the plane.

"Maybe in another life," she shouted out to him. "Oh, I almost forgot. Got some good news," Anya said.

Mac turned. "Yeah?"

"Guo and his men captured Ping."

"What are they going to do with him?"

"They wouldn't give me any details, but I get the feeling his life will be cut short."

"Couldn't happen to a nicer guy." Mac climbed the airplane stairs. Before he entered, he faced her with a broad smile and waved. His smile faded and he disappeared inside.

Tears welled up. She wiped her face as Stahl sidled up next to her.

"I'm glad he abandoned his mission." Stahl sighed. "It would have been a waste to have killed him."

"Funny how quickly things change." Anya said. "Dai Li is now working with the U.S. government.

Stahl said, "Maybe one day he and Mac might work together."

"God forbid."

Stahl handed Anya an envelope.

"What's this?"

"It's from your boss." Stahl let out a guttural laugh and sauntered away.

She watched him for a moment, then removed a piece of paper from the envelope and unfolded it.

MORE ABOUT RED ASSCHER

P. C. Chinick's first thriller in the Red Asscher series, *Living in Fear,* received a Gold medal for best thriller from Global Ebook Awards, a Silver from BellaOnline, and was a Winner for *Scintillating Starts* from the online magazine Writer Advice.

Works are underway on the third installment of the Red Asscher series, *Living in War.*

You can read more about Anya Pavlovitch's story at www.redasscher.com/blog.